HERO

JENNIFER LI SHOTZ

HARPER

An Imprint of HarperCollins*Publishers*

Hero
Copyright © 2016 by Alloy Entertainment

All rights reserved. Printed in the United States of America.
No part of this book may be used or reproduced in any manner whatsoever without
written permission except in the case of brief quotations embodied in critical articles
and reviews. For information address HarperCollins Children's Books, a division of
HarperCollins Publishers, 195 Broadway, New York, NY 10007.
www.harpercollinschildrens.com

Produced by Alloy Entertainment
1325 Avenue of the Americas
New York, NY 10019
www.alloyentertainment.com

Library of Congress Control Number: 2016949975
ISBN 978-0-06-256039-1 (pbk.) — ISBN 978-0-06-256041-4 (trade ed.)
ISBN 978-0-06-265221-8 (paper-over-board)
Typography by Liz Dresner

17 18 19 20 CG/OPM 10 9 8 7 6 5 4 3 2

First Edition

*For my dog-crazy family, and all the Heros, Scouts,
Moussies, and Mangoes in our future*

PROLOGUE

HERO SAT PERFECTLY STILL ON THE auditorium stage, his ears alert, his front paws in alignment. The dog tilted his head ever so slightly and locked his eyes on the police chief, who stood at the podium. From his seat in the front row, Ben thought his chest might burst with pride. Even though he'd known Hero since he was a baby, Ben was still totally blown away by what a great dog Hero was.

Everything about Hero, a black Labrador, was poised and distinguished. Even his thick dark coat was extra shiny—Ben's mom had insisted on taking him to the groomer yesterday. Hero, as usual, had gone without complaint. He even let Ben's little sister, Erin, put a giant bow on his collar. Ben had taken it off that morning before the ceremony. He didn't think Mississippi's most decorated police dog needed to show up for his retirement ceremony with a floppy bow on his neck.

Ben squeezed Erin's tiny hand in his and stood up as straight as he could. Everyone was dressed up for the special occasion, and Ben felt like a man in his new suit. His mom, Jessica, wiped a tear from her eye. She had straightened Ben's tie about a million times that morning before they left the house. Noah, Ben's best friend, fidgeted in his stiff shirt. He was used to playing baseball with Ben, not dressing up—but even he was caught up in the moment.

Ben studied his dad and Hero on the stage at the front of the room. His dad—Sergeant Dave Landry, technically—held Hero's leash in one hand. The badges and medals on his dad's dress uniform glinted every time the photographer's flash went off. His dad wore a serious expression, but Ben could see that his eyes were a little damp too.

Hero was more than just a regular police dog in the K-9 unit—he was also trained as a search-and-rescue dog. Hero and Ben's dad had been partners on the Gulfport police force for eight years. In that time, Hero had busted a lot of criminals—and saved a lot of lives.

Including Ben's.

When Ben was only six, he had wandered away from the house and walked a couple of miles along a nearby creek. He threw small rocks in the air, then swung at them with sticks—playing "baseball." He was so caught up in his game that he didn't realize the sun was going down until he looked up and it was dark. He didn't know which way was home. Ben was terrified. Every tree looked exactly the same, and he couldn't see the path.

He tried to find his way back, but he only got more lost. Finally he sank down at the base of a tree, pulled his arms into his T-shirt for warmth, and sobbed. He thought he would never see his family again.

Then, all of a sudden, Hero had bounded through the darkness and found Ben. The dog had licked the tears right off his face. Even though it was almost seven years later, Ben could still remember the feel of Hero's warm fur in the cold night.

Ben and his family had never forgotten that Hero saved Ben's life. And apparently, neither had Hero: After that night in the woods, whenever Hero and Ben were together, Hero followed Ben everywhere—like he was protecting him.

Every chance he got, Ben's dad would bring Hero to the house to visit Ben. The dog always went straight upstairs to Ben's room, where he'd sit for hours and patiently listen to Ben explain the rules of baseball. For Ben, it was like a dream come true: his two favorite things—Hero and baseball—together in one place.

"We owe Hero a great debt," the police chief said into the microphone. "This town has never seen such a skilled police dog. We can't even count the number of people he's saved or bad guys he's caught. But we can say that every time he was on the job, he amazed us. After a tornado tore up part of our town two years ago, Hero was the first one on the job every morning, and the last to leave at night. He knew every nook and cranny of the rubble, and he saved the lives of several of our friends and neighbors who were buried under the ruins of their own houses."

The chief looked down at Hero appreciatively. "I watched them pull a man out of the destruction," the chief went on. "A man who feared he might never see daylight again. Well, he is alive today because of Hero. I am humbled by this great creature."

There wasn't a dry eye in the room.

"And now," the chief said, "after many years of

service to our community, it's time for Hero to enjoy himself a little. We're sad to see him go, of course, but we feel like Hero has earned the chance to retire and not have to show up to work every day, like the rest of us." The crowd laughed. The chief stepped forward and hung a wide ribbon around the dog's neck. At the end of it dangled a shiny round medal. "Hero, on behalf of the city of Gulfport, Mississippi, I am proud to award you this Medal of Honor for distinguished service. Thank you, sir."

Hero thumped his long, curving tail. He tilted his head up at the chief and let out a little *woof*. Then he opened his mouth and panted a little.

"Look!" Erin cried. "Hero is smiling!"

Ben, his parents, his sister, and Noah all cheered. The rest of the room burst into applause.

Ben's dad stepped down from the small stage, and Hero loped along after him. Ben, his mom, and his sister encircled them in a big group hug.

After a moment, Ben dropped to his knees and wrapped his arms around Hero's neck.

"I'm gonna miss you, pal," he said. The group went quiet. The day was a celebration, but it was also bittersweet. Like most retired police dogs in the area, Hero was going to work for a private security company, doing some light duty. They didn't know how often—or if—they'd get to see him. Ben stood up.

"Sorry," he said sheepishly. "I didn't mean to bring everybody down."

Ben's dad exchanged a look with Ben's mom. She nodded. His dad turned and looked Ben square in the eye. Without a word, he handed Ben the loop at the end of Hero's leash.

"Hero is yours now, son," Ben's dad said.

"Wait—what do you mean?" Ben asked in total surprise.

"You're growing up," his dad said. "And we feel like you're ready to take on more responsibility."

Ben tried to understand what his dad was saying. "Are you serious? You're saying that Hero is really my dog?"

His dad nodded.

"But what about the security company—" Ben asked.

"Not Hero," his dad replied. "This is a good dog who has saved a lot of lives. And one of those lives was pretty important to me. The department knows how special Hero is to our family. They agreed that he deserves only the best, and that means he gets to come live with the Landry family. Taking care of Hero will be your opportunity to show us what you're made of."

"Yes!" Ben blurted out. "I mean, okay, Dad. I can do that . . . I'll do that." Ben was too excited to think, let alone speak. Hero was his!

He looked at Noah to see if he was hearing this or if Ben was just dreaming the whole thing. Noah wore a huge, happy grin and high-fived him. "Now you'll have someone to catch your fly balls, Ben!" his best friend teased.

Ben's mom hugged him tight. "But listen, honey," his mom said. "To keep Hero, you have to keep your grades up and not fall behind in any classes."

"Absolutely, Mom."

"And do all your chores."

"I promise I'll do them, Mom. I'll do anything!"

His parents looked at him with a funny expression on their faces. Like a mixture of pride and happiness, plus a tiny drop of weepiness, all at once.

Ben knew it would be more work than he was used to—taking care of a dog wasn't always easy, and taking care of a hero dog meant that much more pressure. His stomach felt jittery.

He smiled to cover his nerves.

"I know you can do it, Ben," his mom said. She squeezed his shoulders.

"Thanks, Mom," Ben said, hoping she was right.

Ben looked down at Hero, who sat patiently, his medal draped across his soft black chest. Hero snapped his mouth shut and tilted his head back to look at Ben. Ben put his hand on the dog's head. *His* dog's head, he reminded himself. It felt warm and solid under his palm. In his other hand, he gripped the leash. The leather rope felt heavy—full of promise and responsibility. Hero nudged Ben's hand and gave his fingers a lick. It was almost like Hero understood who his new owner was.

Ben wanted to pinch himself. Hero was coming home with him for good.

As they walked to the car, Hero moved with precision, keeping perfect pace with Ben. Lean yet muscular, Hero was a big dog, but in total control of his body. Ben wanted to try something out. He stopped short. The dog stopped at almost exactly the same instant and immediately sat down at Ben's side. Ben stepped forward quickly. Hero hopped up and moved in step with him. Ben stopped; Hero froze and sat down in one fluid motion. *It's like he knows I'm going to stop before I do it,* Ben thought.

Ben's dad was walking a few feet ahead of them. He turned around and watched Ben and Hero over his shoulder. "He's good, right, son?"

Ben nodded in amazement. "No kidding, Dad. How does he do it?"

His dad chuckled. "He just does. It's what he's trained to do, but he was born that way. Hero has always been a natural."

Ben leaned down and touched his nose to Hero's. Hero snuffled Ben's face and looked up at him with big brown eyes.

"It's you and me now, Hero," Ben said with a grin.

1

THE BALL ARCED THROUGH THE AIR and came down fast. Hero pumped his legs and hurtled across the grass, his stride long and graceful, but strong. One minute he had four paws on the ground, the next he was sailing upward, closing his jaw around the ball. He landed effortlessly, taking the impact on his hind legs. He wasn't even panting.

"Did you see that?" Ben shouted at Noah.

"He's amazing," Noah said, shading his eyes to watch Hero race back with the baseball. "He's like half-bird, half-dog."

Ben never got tired of hitting balls for Hero. And Hero never seemed to get tired of chasing them down.

But the only person who loved playing ball more than Ben and Hero combined was Noah. This year, Ben and Noah were determined to make the seventh-grade varsity team. They came with Hero to the baseball park every day after school to practice throwing, hitting, and catching, and to give each other pointers.

Hero bounded back toward them, a slobbery ball perched in his mouth.

"What time is it?" Noah asked.

Ben looked up and noticed that the sun had sunk lower in the sky.

"Four thirty," he said.

"I have to get going," Noah said.

"Yeah, us too. C'mon, Hero. Time to pack it in," Ben said as he gave Hero a scratch on the head.

Hero dropped the ball at Ben's feet. Ben flashed Hero the hand signal for *stay*. Hero stood still. Ben was still mastering all the signals and verbal commands his dad had been using with Hero for years. There wasn't much need for Ben to give Hero the special ones, like *search* and *track*. But Hero knew other commands that would be fun to use, like when to start and stop, whether to run or jump, when to turn around and come back. Hero could stop walking mid-step, if he got the right command. Hero's training was at an expert level—and he always followed orders. That's what a police dog did best.

The dog fixed his serious eyes on Ben. His left ear twitched. He cocked his head to the right. Ben was learning his every expression and gesture.

"You see that look he gives me?" Ben asked Noah. He nodded. "That means he wants me to throw one more ball."

"Wow. Your dog is not only a hero, but he can talk too?" Noah looked down at Hero. Hero wagged his tail.

Ben rolled his eyes. "No, seriously," he said. "If he goes like this"—Ben bobbed his head up and down, doing his best dog impersonation—"he needs to go out to, you know, do his business. If his head moves around like this"—Ben twitched his head to the left, then right, then back again—"he hears something outside. Like he's on watch or something."

Noah looked like he couldn't believe what he was seeing.

"Ben, are you seriously acting like your dog right now?"

Ben shrugged. "Maybe."

Noah dropped to one knee. He held Hero's head in

his hands. "Keep an eye on him for me, okay, Hero? If he starts to become more beast than boy, let me know."

Hero licked him on the nose. Noah laughed and scratched him behind the ears.

"See ya, pal." He stood up and hopped on his bike. "Ben, hit a few more balls, would you? I know I don't need to remind you, but tryouts are in two weeks. And we both have to make varsity or it won't be half as much fun."

Ben grimaced. "No pressure, though, right?"

"Right. For real, though, Ben," Noah said, suddenly serious. "I know you've worked really hard to play short-stop. But you know how Coach is—he's not going to just give it to you. You need to show him. You need to be ready for tryouts."

"I will be." Ben gave his best friend a confident smile.

"Okay. We can practice more tomorrow. You need to tighten up that follow-through." Noah pedaled off. "Bye," he called out over his shoulder.

"Bye." Ben sighed. Most of the time it was great when your best friend was baseball obsessed. But some-times it was just stressful.

Hero watched Ben, furrowing his brow and wrin-kling the soft patch of fur between his eyes.

"Okay, boy," Ben said. "One more ball."

Ben hefted the ball up and down a couple of times. Hero's pointy ears pricked forward, and he dropped into a crouch. His whole body was ready for the chase. Ben let him wait for a long moment, enjoying Hero's excitement. The dog was so . . . alert. If Ben so much as twitched his pinkie finger, Hero noticed. It was like Hero's whole body and mind were in sync, absorbing everything around him. Whatever Hero did, he did wholly and intentionally. That's what Ben needed to do. His dad called it "acting with purpose."

"Slow down, Ben," his dad would say as Ben raced by on his way to his room to do his homework, or to baseball practice, or to an early morning Newspaper Club meeting at school. Ben just powered ahead, without thinking things through. It was the same with baseball. He wasn't the most precise player. He just hit the baseball as hard as he could.

Ben heard his dad's voice in his head. "Slooooow it down. Breathe. Act with purpose, kid. That's how cops do it."

Hero whimpered, as if to say, *Let's get on with it!* Focusing as hard as he could, Ben lifted the bat over his right shoulder and tossed the ball straight up in the air.

He swung. The ball cracked against the bat, then flew up and out—way, way out.

"Whoa!" Ben yelled. He couldn't believe how far he'd hit it. It would definitely have been a home run!

Hero went from standing totally still to galloping after the ball. Ben had no idea how he could get moving so fast. The ball landed in the grass with a thunk.

Ben took off after Hero and caught up to him on the other side of the baseball field, where the park began to give way to heavy woods. Hero pressed his nose to the ground, his nostrils flaring with short, quick inhalations. The ball wasn't there. Hero zigzagged, following his nose, then stopped and sniffed repeatedly in one spot. Spring wildflowers were just beginning to jut out of the grass under Hero's giant paws.

"Where is it, buddy?" Ben asked.

Hero kept his attention on the ground. He walked slowly toward the tree line.

"What do you smell?" Ben followed him. Hero picked up speed and started to head deeper into the woods, where the trees were close together and the undergrowth was thick. *How could the ball have traveled this far?* Ben wondered. Something was different about Hero's movements—he was completely focused.

His ears pointed forward. His nose was working double time. His tail, which usually curved down by his back legs, was up. Even his fur seemed to be paying attention.

Hero was tracking.

Ben had never seen Hero lock onto a scent like this before. He was in full search-and-rescue mode . . . but for what? A baseball? That seemed weird.

Ben was excited to watch Hero in action, but he was not excited to be late for dinner. They were going to have to hurry this along.

"Hero, buddy, my mom is going to kill me if we're late again." Hero pressed his nose into the grass. "It's just a baseball, dude," Ben said. "It'll still be here tomorrow."

Ben was about to give Hero the *stop* command, when suddenly Hero's head shot up. He took off at a full sprint around a dense cluster of trees. Ben sighed. He watched Hero run and then come to a sudden halt. Hero stood as still as a statue, watching something intently in the leaves and vines on the ground. A soft *woof* came from his throat. Ben jogged after him.

"What is it . . ." Ben trailed off. There was his baseball. But how? Out of the corner of his eye, Ben saw a flash of movement—a blur of brown and white leaping over the ball. Hero and Ben watched as the blur tumbled and rolled and pounced. It stopped moving and sat up, the ball gripped firmly in its teeth.

It was . . . a puppy?

2

OVERSIZED BROWN EYES GAZED UP AT them, filled with fear, looking from Hero to Ben and back again. The eyes were set in the face of a tiny, fuzzy puppy. His fur was a golden brown, and he had a black snout, two white paws, and a white chest. One ear pointed straight up, and the other flopped down over his cheek. The dog's nose was twitching, working overtime to take in the new scents of Ben and Hero.

Hero barked. With a frantic yip, the puppy scooted backward and bumped into a wide tree trunk. Trapped, he began to whimper, and his small body shook uncontrollably. He kept his eyes locked on Hero and Ben.

"Hero, quiet. It's okay, pup," Ben said softly, trying

to sound as calm and friendly as possible. "What're you doing way out here?"

Ben knelt down and held out his hand. The puppy eyed his fingers but stayed where he was. Ben took a closer look at the little guy. His fur was dirty and matted. He had a deep scratch across his nose that was starting to heal, and a couple of patches of dried blood on his back. It looked like the pup had been bitten and maybe even clawed. And he was skinny—too skinny. Ben could see his ribs. He definitely hadn't been getting enough to eat.

Ben slipped his backpack off his shoulder slowly, trying not to startle the puppy. He unzipped it and pulled out the remains of a ham sandwich he hadn't finished at lunch. Ben unwrapped the soggy parcel and held it out in one hand. *Do dogs even like ham sandwiches?* he wondered. The puppy caught a whiff, and his straggly tail wagged back and forth in the grass.

"Come on, boy," Ben said softly. The pup took one, then another, tentative step forward, desperate for the food. Ben broke off a small piece of ham and tossed it into the grass. The puppy looked up at Ben, then at Hero, then back down at the food. He lunged forward, snatching the meat from the ground. He looked at Ben, ready for more. Ben tossed another small piece into the grass. The pup gobbled it up. Ben smiled and dropped the rest of the sandwich right at his own feet. The puppy scampered over and scarfed it down.

"When was the last time you had anything to eat?" Ben said quietly. The puppy looked up at him and whimpered as he swallowed the last of the sandwich. "Sorry, pal," Ben said. "I don't have any more."

The puppy dropped to the ground, rolled onto his back, and flopped from side to side, snorting a little. Hero watched the puppy wiggle for a moment. He looked up at Ben, waiting for a command. Ben shrugged.

"You want to check him out, huh, Hero?" Hero just blinked at Ben. "All right." Ben sighed. "Go on, Hero."

Hero stepped over and sniffed at the smaller dog. The puppy lay still on his back, resting a paw on Hero's snout while Hero sized him up from head to tail and back again. Next to Hero, the small dog looked even tinier. He was hardly bigger than Hero's head.

Ben saw another wound on the dog's stomach. This one definitely looked like a bite mark. Ben's dad had mentioned something about stray dogs showing up in the area with these kinds of injuries lately. The police had been able to catch a couple of them and said they were probably being used in a dogfighting ring. This guy was way too little to be a fighter, but maybe he was being used as a bait dog, to get the bigger, meaner dogs riled up.

And if he was, did that mean this puppy belonged to whoever ran the ring? Or had he just been dumped out on the street when they were done with him? Ben wasn't sure which option was worse.

Hero raised his head from the pup. The little dog clambered to his feet and nipped at Hero's neck. Hero ignored the bite and nudged at the puppy with his snout. The little dog dropped back down onto his belly and lowered his head while Hero licked him, cleaning his face and neck.

"Aw, Hero, that's nice of you, buddy," Ben said.

The puppy had his eyes closed and was totally relaxed. Hero lay down on the grass right next to the puppy and scanned the woods around them, as if he were on watch. Ben had to laugh—Hero was protecting the puppy the way he usually protected Ben.

"Well, look at you two," Ben said. "It's like you've known each other forever, huh?"

Ben studied the dogs. Even though they were different colors and had different markings, the puppy kind of looked like Hero. His head was the same rectangular shape, with the same long snout. And the puppy's paws were huge—a giveaway that he'd be as big as Hero someday. He was probably a mutt, but he definitely had some Labrador in him.

"Where's your family, little guy?" Ben asked. He slowly reached out his hand. He waited for the pup to sniff his knuckles, like his dad had taught him. But the little dog pulled his head away, keeping his distance. He was obviously afraid of people, but he felt comfortable with Hero. Someone must have been really mean to him.

The pup tipped his head to the side and sniffed at Ben's backpack, probably hoping for more food. Ben felt terrible, but he and Hero needed to get home. They were going to have to leave the puppy here.

"Come on, Hero," Ben said. Hero looked at him but didn't get up. "Hero, come. We have to get home." Hero didn't budge. Ben had never seen him ignore a command before. "We'll come back tomorrow with some more food for the puppy," Ben said, "but if we don't get home now, my parents are going to kill us. Come."

Hero stood up, but he looked down at the puppy and started to whine. The puppy hopped up and tucked himself between Hero's front legs, under his chest. Both dogs looked up at Ben.

Ben couldn't believe what he was seeing. Was Hero refusing to leave without the puppy? He looked from one dog to the other while he tried to figure out what to do.

"Uh, Hero, my parents are going to be mad at me if we're late. What do you think they're going to do if I'm late and I bring home another dog?" The dogs just stared at him. Ben shook his head. "Oh, man. Okay, okay. We'll take the puppy home with us."

Ben pulled Hero's harness out of his backpack and put it down on the ground. Carefully, he adjusted the buckles to make it as small as possible. He held up the harness and reached for the puppy, but the little dog let out a high-pitched growl and backed away from Ben. Hero nudged the puppy toward Ben with his nose. The pup stumbled reluctantly forward, Hero right behind him.

Ben slowly stretched his hands out again. This time the pup sniffed him and the harness. Ben gently lowered the harness over the pup's head. He swiped one tiny paw at the nylon straps and scooted backward, trying to get out of it. Hero licked the puppy's head, as if to reassure him that it was okay. After a moment, the pup accepted the harness and sat down. It was loose, but it would work.

Ben turned to Hero. "You happy now, bud?"

Hero wagged his tail and let out a short, happy bark.

"I thought you'd say that." Ben clipped Hero's leash to the harness. He tugged on it lightly. The puppy resisted and tried to bite the strap. Ben tugged again. "Okay, pal. Up you go." The puppy stood, and Hero rose to his feet, standing at Ben's side.

"I think he needs a name, don't you, Hero?" Ben looked at the pup, then back at Hero. Ben thought of all the people his dog had saved over the years. He thought of how Hero could sniff out trouble and find people in danger. He thought of all the times Hero and his dad had put their lives on the line to help others.

Maybe the puppy belonged to someone else, and maybe they would have him only for a day. But Hero had tracked the pup into the woods—had saved him—and instantly taken a liking to him. It was almost like the pup was a tiny version of the older dog. And what was Hero? A searcher . . . a rescuer . . . Ben ran through all the words that popped into his head until he came to the right one.

"Scout," Ben said quietly, trying out the name. It felt right. "Scout," he repeated, louder this time.

Ben started walking. Hero followed, and Scout waddled along behind them. The little dog took four wiggling steps for every one of Hero's, his short legs working overtime.

"Come on, Hero. Come on, Scout," Ben said to the pair. "We're going home."

3

THEY MADE IT HOME JUST IN time for dinner. At the sight of his parents' cars in the driveway, Ben felt a twinge of uncertainty in his gut. On the ride home, with Hero trotting alongside his bike and Scout tucked into the front of Ben's sweatshirt, Ben had gotten pretty comfortable with the idea of bringing the puppy home. It wouldn't have been right to leave the tiny dog there alone at night. And clearly Hero wasn't going to allow that to happen. But now what? He had no plan. In fact, he hadn't thought this through at all, beyond getting home on time. What would they do with Scout? Would his parents even let him bring the dog inside?

Ben hopped off his bike and dropped it on the front

lawn. He raced up the walkway, carrying Scout under one arm in a football hold. Nervously, he opened the front door.

His dad was in the kitchen cooking dinner. He heard the clatter of a pan lid and his dad muttering, "Ow, that was hot." His sister, Erin, sat at the dining room table, clutching a crayon in her pudgy hand. Erin and Ben were six years apart in age, but they looked almost identical, with the same freckles, light brown eyes, and curly brown hair. His mom stood in front of the couch in the adjoining living room, folding laundry into neat piles. All three of them looked up and immediately spotted Scout in Ben's arms.

Erin jumped out of her seat and ran toward him, squealing, "Puppy!" at the top of her lungs.

Oh, his mom mouthed in surprise. His dad squinted as if trying to decide whether it was a real dog. Scout started to tremble with fear in Ben's arms. He looked around anxiously, taking in all the new faces and sounds and smells. Erin held out her hand to Scout, who sniffed at it nervously.

"It's okay, boy," Ben said softly, patting Scout's head. "That's just my kid sister. She won't bite." Erin stuck her tongue out at Ben.

Ben looked to his mom and saw a glimmer of appreciation for Scout's cuteness cross her face. He held Scout out toward her. "He's a little nervous, but he's really sweet, Mom. Want to hold him?"

"No thanks," his mom replied, shaking her head. "At least not until he's had a bath and a flea dip."

"So," his dad said, with an amused expression on his face. "What exactly are you planning to do with that dog?"

"Um." Ben didn't know where to start. "We—Hero and I—I mean, I . . . Scout was all alone. The puppy was all alone. We found him in the woods at the park. Hero wouldn't let me leave him there. I mean—Hero really liked him right away. He's such a little guy."

His dad nodded. "He is. He's just a pup. A really cute pup." Ben's dad walked toward them. He was tall—well over six feet—and he towered over Ben and Scout. Scout tried to push himself backward in Ben's arms, like he was trying to get away from his dad.

"It's okay, Scout," Ben said softly. Hero stood up on his hind legs and put his front legs on Ben's arm. He licked Scout on the face, soothing him. Scout immediately relaxed in Ben's arms.

"Hero really does like him, huh?" Ben's dad said. He studied Scout carefully. Ben's dad loved dogs. He was the best officer in the K-9 unit. Ben could tell that his dad wanted to keep Scout too. But Ben's mom would be the ultimate decider. "He's got some bite marks on him," Ben's dad said as he ran a gentle hand over Scout's trembling body. "His wounds are consistent with the other dogs we've found in town lately. I'd bet my next paycheck this little guy is part of the same fighting ring."

"I was afraid of that," Ben said. "So, can we keep him?" He held his breath and looked at his parents. He hadn't realized until that very moment that he actually wanted to keep Scout. He already had one dog. Now he wanted two?

Ben saw his parents share a look. Erin bounced up and down on her toes, practically bursting with excitement. Scout let out a hungry whimper in Ben's arms.

"What did you call him?" Ben's dad asked.

"Scout," Ben said, kind of embarrassed. "Because he reminds me of Hero."

"Honey," Ben's mom interrupted. "Let's talk this over, please?" She smiled and shook her head. Ben's dad shot her a sheepish look.

"Well, take Scout out back and hose him down while your mom and I discuss what to do with him," his dad said.

"Sure thing," Ben said, happy that his parents hadn't given him an outright *no*.

"There are some old towels and Hero's dog shampoo in the laundry room," Ben's mom called after him as Ben and the dogs headed outside.

"Thanks, Mom." Ben gave Scout a scratch behind the ears.

"Can I help?" Erin asked.

"Sure," Ben said. "Come on."

Ben had never given a puppy a bath before—it was more like the puppy gave him and Erin a bath. They hosed him off as best as they could, then stepped back into the kitchen half an hour later dripping wet and muddy from chasing the slippery dog across the lawn. At least Scout was clean and wrapped in a snuggly towel.

"Upstairs!" Ben's mom commanded them both with a laugh. "Get those wet clothes out of here."

Ben put the pup down on the floor, and Hero immediately walked over and lay down next to him.

When Ben came back downstairs in dry clothes, he found his parents watching the two dogs on the floor. Hero had his front paws stretched out in front of him and his ears pricked forward, on alert. Scout leaned against Hero's side and licked himself. The downy fur on the backs of his ears stuck out in all directions.

"I'm surprised that Hero is so attached to this puppy," Ben's dad said. "I've never seen him like this before."

"Yeah," Ben said. "He wasn't going to come home without Scout. He made that pretty clear."

"Well," Ben's dad said, "Hero's not going to like this, but your mom and I have decided that Scout needs to go to the shelter tonight."

Ben's heart sank.

"Then tomorrow," his dad went on, "when I get to the station, I'll see if anyone's filed a missing dog report. There's a chance Scout could be someone's pet, although, like I said, I suspect he was part of the dogfighting ring. If he was, he might be able to help me find out who's behind it and put an end to it once and for all. Either way, they'll take good care of him at the shelter."

"But, Dad—"

"Sorry, Ben. It's the right thing to do. I'll run him over there now while your mom finishes making dinner." He leaned down to scoop up Scout from the floor. As he did, Scout skittered backward, away from Ben's dad, a frightened wail escaping his throat. Scout had gotten comfortable with Ben pretty quickly, and he had let Erin hold him right away. But something about Ben's dad terrified the puppy.

Hero buried his nose in the pup's fur, comforting him.

Ben's dad took another step toward Scout, and Hero stood up, positioning himself between the man and the puppy.

"Whoa, Hero," Ben's dad said, surprised. "It's okay, pal. I'm not going to hurt him. Sit."

Hero sat, but he kept his eyes locked on his longtime handler. Scout trembled with fear, but he let Ben's dad pick him up and head for the front door. Before Ben's dad could get there, though, Hero bounded across the room and stepped in front of him.

"Hero really doesn't want you to take him," Ben's mom said, astonished.

"I guess not," Ben's dad replied.

"That's how Hero was acting in the woods," Ben said, hoping the dog could convince his parents to let Scout stay.

Still cradling Scout in his arms, Ben's dad reached for the doorknob. Hero barked at him. It wasn't an aggressive bark, but it was clear from Hero's tone and furrowed brow that he was upset. He started to whine.

Ben's dad took a step backward, away from the door.

Hero stopped whining and wagged his tail. Ben's dad took a step forward again, and Hero barked. Ben's dad studied Hero for a moment.

"You're not kidding, are you, Hero?" He looked back at his wife. Ben's mom raised her hands in an *I don't know* gesture. "What do you think, hon?" Ben's dad asked her.

"I think Hero knows what he wants." She sighed. "It sounds like Scout stays."

"Dad?" Ben asked, his heart thumping in his chest.

"All right," his dad said.

"Yes!" Ben pumped a fist in the air. "Thanks, Mom. Thanks, Dad."

"This isn't permanent, Ben," his dad cautioned. "Tomorrow I'll figure out where Scout came from, and we'll get him back where he belongs. As long as it's safe for him there."

Ben nodded. "I understand. But good luck explaining that to Hero." He chuckled.

"No kidding," his dad replied. "Listen, no matter how attached Hero is to the puppy, we don't know this dog at all. I know this is hard to hear, but dogs like this—they've usually been treated pretty badly. Sometimes people are awful to animals. And it . . . changes them."

"I know, Dad."

"Plus, you don't have a lot of time to take care of a puppy, Ben," his mom chimed in. "You've got to keep your grades up in order to keep Hero, remember?"

He remembered. How could he forget?

"Two dogs and school," his mom went on, "that's a ton of responsibility. And a puppy is a lot more work than a well-trained dog like Hero."

"I'll help!" Erin shrieked. "Are you hungry, puppy?" She ran for the cabinet, grabbed a bowl, and filled it with Hero's kibble. She dropped it on the floor next to Hero's bowl, ran to her dad, and snatched Scout from his hands. The puppy looked completely confused.

"Easy, Erin!" Ben cried, cringing. But once he caught a whiff of the food, Scout didn't seem to mind. He went floppy in her arms, his back legs dangling and his tail wagging.

Erin carried the puppy across the room and set him down in front of the bowl. Scout went right to work, crunching away at the kibble.

Ben whipped out his phone and texted Noah: *Wait till you see what I found today*. He couldn't wait for Noah to meet Scout.

4

LATER THAT NIGHT, BEN TOOK THE dogs into the backyard to run them around before bed. He gently lobbed a ball across the lawn. Hero raced after it, but Scout was busy playing with a stick he had found in the grass. He gripped it between his teeth and waved it around in a big figure eight.

Hero leaped up and snatched the ball out of the air. He carried it over to Scout. As Hero approached, Scout dropped the stick and wagged his tail. Hero deposited the ball at the puppy's feet and nudged it toward him with his nose. Scout picked it up and commenced chewing on it.

"Aw, Hero," Ben said. "That was nice of you, pal. Bring me the ball, Scout!"

Scout looked at Ben but didn't move.

"Come on, Scout! Bring me the ball." Ben patted his thigh with his palm to summon the dog over. Confused, Scout dropped the ball on the grass. Hero instantly picked it up and carried it over to Ben. Then Hero looked back at Scout, as if to say, *See?*

Ben took the ball. "Just like that, okay, Scout? Let's try it again." Ben lofted the ball gently into the air toward Scout. Scout saw the airborne object heading toward him and startled. He leaped sideways as quickly as he could.

"It's okay, Scout," Ben called out. "It's not going to hurt you."

But Scout wasn't buying it. He crouched in the grass, his eyes locked on the ball as it landed on the ground a few feet away from him. Only after the ball came to a complete stop did Scout run over and tackle it.

Ben's dad came outside to watch the dogs in action.

"Do you think Scout's afraid of the ball because it's moving," Ben asked his dad, "or because I threw it?"

"Hard to say. Try it again," his dad replied.

At the sound of the grown man's voice, Scout's head snapped up. The puppy eyed Ben's dad with suspicion.

"What's wrong with him, Dad?" Ben asked, his voice tinged with worry.

"He's so young," Ben's dad said, shaking his head. "If a big man made him fight bigger dogs . . ." He trailed off. "That can imprint on a little pup like that forever. Safe bet the people who did that to him were men, like me. I can't really blame Scout for his less-than-trusting attitude."

Hero nosed at Scout and gently tipped him over sideways, then commenced licking the puppy's fur.

Ben couldn't imagine who would do that to such a young puppy—or to any dog, really. It made him sad to think about how scared and lonely Scout had already felt in his short life. First he was treated terribly; then he was all alone in the woods. No wonder he was so skittish.

"Go on," Ben's dad said. "Throw the ball for him again."

Ben took the ball from Scout. He walked back to his original spot and held the ball out in front of him. Scout followed it with his eyes. Very gently, Ben rolled the ball on the grass. As it approached Scout, he leaped to his feet and scooted backward, a growl escaping his throat.

The ball stopped, and Scout sniffed at it. He swatted at it with one paw.

"He's just a real nervous pup," Ben's dad said.

"What can I do to help him?" Ben asked.

His dad exhaled slowly, thinking. "It's possible that with some good training and a safe environment, Scout could be less jumpy. And he might get more comfortable with people, especially men."

"Really?" Ben asked excitedly. "Do you mean regular training like 'sit' and 'stay' and stuff? Or can we teach him some search-and-rescue commands?"

"Well, remember, we don't know how long he's going to be here with us. But no matter what, don't get your hopes up too high, Ben. I can't say for sure that anything will help. This dog has been through some pretty rough stuff. He's got some trust issues."

"It can't hurt to try, though, right?" Ben asked.

"Not at all," his dad said. He grinned and tipped his head toward Hero. "Assuming the boss dog is okay with it. How does that sound, Hero?"

Hero gave a soft *woof* and began panting. It looked like there was a smile on his face.

Ben hated that Scout was so anxious. He had to do something to help the puppy feel better. He crossed the lawn and squatted down next to the dogs.

"Okay, Scout," Ben said, "we're gonna learn a few

moves. You ready?" Scout flopped over onto his back.

Ben ran into the kitchen and grabbed some of Hero's treats from the bag on the counter. When Ben got back outside, both dogs caught the scent immediately and jumped up.

"Come here, Scout!" From his spot on the grass, Scout cocked his head and looked at Ben, his ears flopping a little. "Come here, boy!" Ben repeated. He held out the treat and waved it in the air. Scout stood up and trotted toward Ben. Hero stayed put but watched Ben and Scout intently.

"Attaboy," Ben said soothingly. "Good boy, Scout. Okay. Now you need to learn to sit. *Sit*," he said firmly, pushing down on Scout's backside at the same time. "*Sit*," Ben repeated.

Scout lay down on his tummy and wagged his tail. He let out a short yip. He rolled over onto his back and thrust all four paws into the air. He barked again. He did everything but sit.

Ben and his dad laughed.

Hero hopped up and walked over to Scout. The bigger dog stood right next to Scout, looked at Ben, and wagged his tail. Ben couldn't believe it—Hero was waiting for Ben to give him the *sit* command so he could demonstrate to Scout what he was supposed to do.

"Is Hero doing what I think he's doing, Dad?"

His dad nodded. "He sure is. Apparently our Hero is now a teacher."

"Okay, Scout," Ben said. "Watch Hero. Hero, sit."

Hero sat, his front paws placed close together, his legs straight. He waited patiently for the treat, which Ben held out on his palm.

"See, Scout? That's sitting."

Scout watched, looking from Hero to Ben's palm and back again. Ben and Hero repeated the command a couple of times. Scout's whole body started to wiggle with anticipation.

"Your turn," Ben said to the puppy. "Scout, sit."

Scout barked. He bolted a few feet away, then zig-zagged back. An energetic fluff ball, Scout flopped down onto the grass right next to Hero.

Ben laughed. "Okay, we're getting there, I guess? Let's try it again. Hero, sit."

Hero sat.

"Scout, *sit*!" Ben said.

Scout sat. Hero barked excitedly.

"Attaboy, Scout!" Ben called out, giving the puppy a treat.

"I've seen Hero take care of other animals before," Ben's dad said, "but nothing like this. A few years back, we tracked a runaway teenager to an old farmhouse where there were a bunch of neglected horses and dogs and ducks. Well, the animal control guys were having some trouble rounding up all the animals, so Hero took it upon himself to help out. He herded this little brood of ducklings around the property, all the way around a pond, and right up to the van like he'd been doing it all his life." Ben's dad chuckled at the memory. "Down at the station, they called him 'Cowboy' for a month."

Scout licked Hero's face. Hero closed his eyes and let the puppy snuffle and snort in his ear.

"Well, Scout may not be a duckling," Ben said, "but Hero is pretty crazy about him."

"Seems that way," his dad said, heading for the back door. "I set up a crate for Scout in the kitchen. Good night, Ben."

"Good night, Dad."

Ben watched Hero and Scout for a few minutes. Hero lay down on the grass, his head resting on his front paws and his eyes closed while Scout clambered up and over his back. Hero's fur twitched as Scout's nails tickled him, and Scout's tail wagged a mile a minute. It was like they had known each other forever—not for just a few hours.

Ben hated to break up the fun, but it was getting late, and he still had homework to do. He took out another treat from his pocket and opened the door to the kitchen.

"Hero, come," he said. Hero hopped up, sending Scout rolling onto the grass, and trotted toward Ben. Scout whimpered and looked after Hero longingly. "Scout, come," Ben said. Scout whined some more and buried his nose in the ground, snorting loudly. Hero walked back to Scout and nudged the puppy with his snout. "Scout, come," Ben repeated. Reluctantly, Scout stood up and waddled over toward Ben.

Ben placed the treat in Scout's crate. Scout stepped right inside and snatched it up. He didn't even flinch when Ben closed the door and latched it. Ben could tell Scout was comfortable being in a cage. He must have had one wherever he'd lived before, Ben figured—and it was probably the safest place he knew.

"Good night, Scout," Ben said, wiggling a finger through the metal bars. Scout lay down on the old towels Ben's mom had put in the crate, along with a water bowl. "Come on, Hero," Ben said. "Let's go upstairs." Hero slept at the foot of Ben's bed every night.

But Hero had plopped down next to Scout's cage, and he was clearly settled in for the night. Ben shook his head in wonder.

"Look at you, Hero," he said, laughing. "You're a goner for this pup. Fine. Good night, pal." He gave Hero one good scratch behind the ears and headed upstairs to his room.

Ben collapsed onto his bed and yawned. It had gotten late, and he still had a couple of hours of homework. He pulled out his books. A handout with a long list of words stuck out from between two of them. Ugh! The vocab quiz in the morning—he'd forgotten about it. He had more work than he'd realized.

On top of the stack of homework was a dog-training book that Ben had checked out of the library. It was written by a former police dog trainer. He'd wanted to learn more about how to give Hero his commands, but maybe it would come in handy for training Scout too.

With a guilty glance at his textbooks and vocab list, Ben flipped it open. *Just for a few minutes,* he promised himself. *I'll do my homework after.* He read the introduction, which talked all about something called positive reinforcement. Instead of focusing on punishing your dog, you were supposed to praise them whenever they did something good.

Ben practiced some of the basic commands—come, stop, roll over. It was almost midnight. He reached for his math notebook and started on the first problem. He just had to solve for x . . . But Ben's eyelids were so heavy. His head too. He just needed some support from the pillow. Just for a few minutes . . .

5

"BEN! ARE YOU STILL ASLEEP UP there?"

Ben bolted upright, confused about why he was fully dressed on his bed. His math notebook was open on his lap, and his pencil had fallen on the floor. The light was on. He'd fallen asleep doing his homework. He checked his alarm clock. He was late for school, and his vocab quiz was first period.

"Ben!"

"Uh—I'm coming, Mom!"

Ben leaped out of bed and changed his clothes as quickly as he could. He threw his backpack over his shoulder and raced downstairs. Hero lay on the kitchen floor, and Scout was out of his crate. Ben zipped past them and dumped some kibble in their bowls. Hero ate slowly, picking up a bite of food and stepping away from his bowl while he chewed it. Scout, on the other hand, scarfed his food down in record time. Out of the corner of his eye, as he grabbed his lunch from the fridge, Ben saw Hero stop eating and push his bowl toward Scout. Scout happily dug into the last of Hero's kibble.

Hero looked over at Ben and wagged his tail, ready for his usual morning walk.

"Sorry, Hero," Ben said. "I'm late for school, but I'll take you for an extra-long walk later, I promise." Hero's tail dropped as Ben headed for the door without him. "Take care of Scout today, okay?"

Ben got to school after the last bell had already rung. He raced down the empty hallway, breathing hard from riding his bike so fast. He pushed on the classroom door too hard. It banged open—and every kid in Mr. Stein's English class looked up from their quiz. So much for a quiet entrance.

"It's not like you to be late for a quiz, Ben," his teacher whispered. "Is everything all right? You can take the quiz after school, okay?"

Ben exhaled with relief. "Thanks, Mr. Stein," he said, catching his breath. "I'm fine. Just late."

Maybe this day wouldn't entirely suck after all.

Ben sank into his seat to wait out the rest of the period. Noah shot him a sympathetic look from his spot across the room. Ben felt someone looking at him and turned to the kid on his right. It was the new guy, Jack, who'd moved to Gulfport last semester, right before the holiday break. Ben made eye contact and nodded. Jack nodded back. Ben had heard a rumor that Jack played shortstop at his old middle school—varsity, no less. Ben also knew that there was only one open spot for shortstop this year, which meant his biggest competition was going to be Jack.

"Jack," Mr. Stein called out from the front of the class. "Keep your eyes to yourself, please."

"Sorry," Jack said. He turned back to his quiz, but not before scowling at Ben. Ben was taken aback—why was Jack mad at him? It wasn't his fault Jack had been staring at him—all Ben had done was look up and nod.

After sixth period, Ben pushed through a steady stream of kids in the hall and back to Mr. Stein's classroom. He hefted his backpack, loaded with heavy textbooks, onto one shoulder. He felt a solid *thwack* as it hit someone, hard.

Ben spun around to see who he'd clobbered with his

books, an apology already spilling from his lips. It was Jack. He stood at his locker, rubbing his shoulder where Ben had hit him.

"Sorry, Jack," Ben said. "I didn't mean to—"

Jack squinted at Ben, his face unreadable. He opened his mouth as if to speak. Ben waited for him to say something, like *It's okay*, or *No worries*. But Jack just stared at him, snapped his mouth shut, and turned back to his open locker without a word.

"Uh . . . okay," Ben muttered to himself. "That was awkward." But he didn't have time to wonder what Jack's problem was—he had to make up his English quiz, which he totally hadn't studied for.

As he hustled toward Mr. Stein's room, Noah appeared at his side.

"What happened to you this morning?"

"I overslept."

"Ben Landry never oversleeps," Noah teased him. "Ben Landry is always on time for, like, everything."

"I stayed up late playing with Scout—the puppy— and Hero."

"If I had a puppy, I'd stay up late too," Noah said, a hint of envy in his voice. "I'm so psyched to meet him."

"Well, you'll have to get approval from Hero first," Ben said. "He's completely nuts about Scout. It's like Scout is the puppy he never had or something."

"Really?" Noah said. "I wouldn't have guessed Hero was the puppy type. Are we still on for training today?" he asked.

"Uh . . ." Ben said.

"Batting practice. Duh."

"Oh, right," Ben replied. His mom had promised to come home and let Scout out of his cage on her lunch break, so he knew the puppy would be fine. "Yes, I'll be there, but I have to take that quiz first."

"Why don't I come over to meet Scout after we hit a few balls?"

"Sure thing. You can help me with him too," Ben said as he stepped into his English classroom.

"Cool," Noah said with a wave.

"I'm really sorry about this morning," Ben said to Mr. Stein as he sat down at a desk. "I've never missed a quiz before."

"I know," the teacher said. "That's why you're getting a second chance. Not everyone would, but you're not the kind of student to take advantage, Ben." Mr. Stein came over and placed the quiz on Ben's desk. Then he wandered back to the front of the classroom and started grading papers.

Ben made his way down the page, yawning and struggling to remember the vocabulary words. Somehow he powered through it. He thanked Mr. Stein as he handed over the piece of paper, and crossed his fingers he wouldn't fail.

The halls were empty and quiet by the time he was done. Ben stepped through the school's heavy front doors and found Hero sitting on the stairs, where he waited for Ben every afternoon. Ben gave the dog a scratch on the head. "Come on, Hero."

Ben hopped on his bike and headed over to the ball field to meet Noah, Hero trotting by his side. Noah wasn't there yet—at least there was one thing Ben hadn't been late for today. He pulled his mitt from his back-pack and started to warm up. He threw the ball deep into the outfield. Hero raced after it, picked it up, and ran it back to him. For the first time since he'd opened his eyes that morning, Ben started to relax.

"Hi," said a boy's voice from behind the backstop.

Ben turned and saw Jack. "Hi," he said.

He wasn't at all sure how he felt about this new kid . . . he couldn't tell if Jack was shy, or rude, or just kind of uncomfortable. But he knew he should try to give Jack the benefit of the doubt. It must be hard to move somewhere new, and Jack probably wanted to be shortstop as badly as Ben. It wasn't Jack's fault they both played the same position. They could be good sports about it.

Hero ran back, the ball clamped firmly between his teeth, and dropped it at Ben's feet. Ben scratched Hero behind the ears and picked up the ball.

"That's a cool dog," Jack said, eyeing Hero intently. "What's his name?"

"Hero," Ben said after a pause. Something felt off about the way Jack watched the dog.

"You want me to pitch to you?" Jack asked Ben. "That seems like it's the one thing your dog can't do."

Ben hesitated. Jack was hot and cold—he'd been weird earlier in the day, but now he suddenly wanted to practice together? Ben felt a little prickle of suspicion, but he pushed the thought away. Plus, there was still no sign of Noah, and he really needed to practice.

"Uh, okay. Sure." Ben wiped the slobber off the ball and handed it to Jack. If *he* was a new kid at a new school, he'd want Jack to treat him with friendship and respect, Ben told himself.

Jack jogged out to the mound and shook out his arm a little. Ben picked up his bat and took a couple of warm-up swings.

"Ready?" Jack called out.

Ben nodded. He raised the bat behind him and bent his knees, dropping into a hitting stance. The ball whizzed toward him. He swung and missed. The kid had a good arm. Hero grabbed the ball and ran it over to Jack.

"Hero, go," Ben said, tilting his head in the direction of the backstop. He didn't want Hero to get hit by a stray ball or foul tip. Hero ran behind the chain-link fence and watched as Ben prepared to swing again.

Jack threw a few more pitches, and Ben got hits off them all. He was feeling pretty good. Noah rode up on his bike and stood behind the backstop with Hero.

"Hey, Ben," he said.

"Hey, Noah," Ben replied without turning around. He was trying to give Jack all his focus.

"Hi, Jack," Noah called out to the boy on the mound.

Jack nodded at Noah but didn't speak to him.

"Let's hit one more," Ben said to Jack. "Then I'm going to practice with Noah, okay?"

"Whatever you want," Jack said. "You warmed up?"

It seemed like a weird question to Ben. Hadn't he just hit a whole bunch of balls? Obviously he was warmed up. Ben lowered his bat and looked at Jack for a minute. He was too far away to be sure, but Ben thought he saw an odd look on the other boy's face. He almost looked . . . disappointed? Was it because Noah was there and Ben was going to practice with him instead?

Ben shook his head. It'd just been a weird day—his mind was playing tricks on him.

"All ready," Ben said. Jack wound up and released the ball. Ben started to swing, but something was wrong. The ball was coming in too fast and too high. It was aimed right at his head.

"Hit the dirt!" Noah yelled from behind him.

Ben's reflexes kicked in faster than his brain could process what was happening. He ducked. The ball was so close to his head that he heard it whiz past his ear and felt it ruffle his hair.

The ball slammed into the chain-link fence behind him, and Hero raced around the front, barking angrily. Noah ran after him and grabbed him by the collar.

Adrenaline shot through Ben's body, followed closely by outrage. He threw the bat down on the ground.

"What was that for?" he yelled at Jack.

"That was lame, Jack!" Noah yelled at the same time. He stood next to Ben, still holding on to Hero. A low growl rumbled in Hero's throat.

"I guess my aim just sucks. Sorry, man." Jack shrugged.

Ben clenched his hands into fists. "Your aim does not suck, dude," he shouted. "Did you just do that on purpose?"

Noah gripped his shoulder with a firm hand.

"You know what, Ben," Noah said, his voice forced into sounding calm. "He's not worth it. Ignore him."

Noah was right. Ben clamped his mouth shut, which wasn't easy. Hero stood close to Ben's side, protecting him. He was still growling.

"Quiet, Hero," Ben said soothingly, resting a hand on his dog's head. "Thanks for looking out for me, pal. Good dog."

"Let's go," Noah said, turning his back on Jack. "I need to meet Scout anyway."

"Okay." Ben picked up his bat. He started to leave, Hero shadowing him.

"Aw, come on—we were just getting started," Jack yelled from the mound. "Let's hit some more. That is, if your dog says it's okay."

Ben shook his head and took a few deep breaths to

calm himself. What was this kid's problem?

"Nah, I'm good, thanks," Ben said through gritted teeth. "I think you've done enough for one day."

"Tell you what," Jack went on. "One more at bat. If I strike you out, I get your dog."

Ben didn't even bother to respond. That was a ridiculous thing for Jack to say. He would never bet Hero for anything—what kind of a person would do something like that?

Without a backward glance, Ben tucked his bat and mitt under his arm and walked off the field with Noah and Hero at his side.

6

BEN TRIED TO PUSH JACK OUT of his mind as he and Noah rode their bikes back to his house. Hero ran next to him.

From the driveway, Ben heard barking and whimpering from inside his house. Hero's ears pricked straight up. Was Scout hurt? Ben raced for the door and opened it. Before he could step through it, Hero squeezed past his legs and ran inside.

Ben froze in the doorway.

"No—no, no, no, no, no," he said, his hands on either side of his head in horror. Ben couldn't believe what he was seeing.

His house had been trashed.

All the couch cushions were on the floor. A roll of paper towels had been completely chewed to bits, cardboard tube and all, and spread across the room. Tiny shreds of paper littered every open surface. One of the chairs from the dining room table had been knocked over. A twenty-pound bag of kibble had been chewed open. Hard little crumbs were everywhere. The tall kitchen garbage can had been tipped over, and its smelly, wet contents strewn across the floor. Several pairs of Ben's shoes lay askew in the middle of the wreckage.

And worst of all, Scout's crate lay on its side, the door hanging open. It was empty.

"Scout?!" Ben called.

Noah stuck his head through the door frame beside him and sucked in his breath.

"Youch," Noah said. "What the heck happened?"

"Scout, did you do this?" Ben demanded, scanning the rubble for the puppy. Scout cowered under the table, shaking. His big, scared eyes looked up at Ben. "Scout!" Anger rose in Ben's chest. *Positive reinforcement,* the dog training book had said. *Don't talk to your dog in anger.* Ben took a couple of deep breaths and tried to figure out how to handle this. What could possibly be positive about this?

Hero *click-clack*ed across the kitchen floor and sniffed at the mess. In control of his emotions now, Ben crossed the room and picked up Scout. He held the puppy's nose close to his own.

"Scout, man, what happened? Are you okay?" Ben said softly to the puppy.

Scout licked Ben on the nose tentatively. The dog still seemed miserable. Ben could relate.

Noah walked over to them and checked out the puppy.

"What's up, Scout?" he said. "Nice to meet you." He turned to Ben and shook his head. "He's cute all right. But he's tiny. How could he possibly have done this much damage?"

"I don't know," Ben replied.

"And why?" Noah said.

It was a good question. Ben tried to envision Scout running around, knocking things over and dragging pillows across the floor. The whole thing was weird—Scout wasn't a hyper dog. He was more scared than anything else.

That was it.

"He must have gotten spooked," Ben said. "He wouldn't have done this otherwise. He's a good dog."

"Spooked? By what?" Noah wondered.

"I have no idea. But whatever it was, he definitely overreacted." Scout was whimpering and wiggling in Ben's arms. Ben looked down and saw that Scout was looking at Hero. He was desperate to get down and go over to the bigger dog.

"He was scared without Hero here," Ben said. "That's why he did this." He put Scout down, and the puppy scuttled across the floor and right under Hero's front legs. He cowered under Hero's chest while Hero surveyed the damage all around them.

Ben looked at the clock on the stove and dropped his head into his hands. "My parents . . . they're going to be home in an hour, and if they see this, there's no way Scout can stay." He looked at Noah pleadingly. "Can you help me? Please? I'm sorry, I know this is, like, seriously gross. But I'll never get it done in time by myself."

Noah laughed.

"What's so funny?" Ben asked. He really didn't see anything amusing about all this.

"Your face. I don't think I've ever seen you so freaked out before."

Ben started laughing too. "I don't know if I've ever felt this freaked out before."

"Of course I'll help you, stupid," Noah said.

They got to work. Ben tried not to gag as he used a wad of paper towels to scoop up a sopping wet pile of kibble mixed with coffee grounds and banana peel.

"Gross," Ben muttered.

"It looks like the world's worst smoothie," Noah said over his shoulder. He was busy picking up the last few tiny fluffs of paper, which floated away from him just as he reached for them. "Come on," he cursed at the scraps. "By the way, where did Scout get all your shoes?"

Ben looked at the pile of his sneakers, then at Scout, who watched them from his safe spot by Hero. "From my closet. Seriously—these were all upstairs. He must have dragged them down one by one."

"That's dedication," Noah said. He snatched a scrap of paper that floated by. "Gotcha."

Ben got out the mop and did a quick pass over the kitchen floor. It wasn't perfect, but it was good enough. They heard the sound of the front door opening. Noah plopped down on the couch. Ben quickly stashed the mop back in the closet and sat down at the table. He pulled a notebook from his backpack and adopted an expression of serious concentration. Noah pulled his math book onto his lap just as Ben's mom and sister stepped into the room.

"Hi, boys!" Ben's mom said.

"Hi, Noah. Hi, Benny," Erin said. She headed straight for Noah and gave him a hug.

"How about a high five?" Noah said, poking Erin in the belly. Erin giggled and slapped his hand.

"How was your day?" Ben's mom said to them.

"Interesting," Ben replied, pretending to be struggling with a math problem.

"Interesting, huh? You'll have to fill me in on that later." His mom turned to Noah. "Can you stay for dinner?"

"Oh, thanks, Mrs. Landry." Noah smiled. "I'd love to, but my mom needs me to help her with some stuff tonight. Something about getting music to play on her phone."

Ben's mom rolled her eyes. "Oh, well, you know us parents and technology."

She started poking through the fridge and pulling things out for dinner. As she turned to throw something in the trash can, she froze. Ben and Noah exchanged a nervous glance.

"Well, how did that get over there?" Ben's mom said to herself.

She nudged the tall pail over a few inches, then

turned back to the food on the counter. Ben exhaled in relief. Noah stifled a laugh.

"I'd better get home," Noah said brightly. "Bye, Erin! Nice to see you, Mrs. Landry."

"You too, dear," Ben's mom said. "Say hi to your mom for me."

"I will." Noah turned to Ben. "Ben, if you have any more trouble with that . . . uh . . . math problem"—Ben rolled his eyes—"just give me a call later."

"I will. Actually, I think Hero and Scout need to go out. Mom, I'll be right back."

Ben followed Noah out the front door and shut it behind them. Hero and Scout bounded across the front lawn.

"Seriously, dude, thank you so much. There's no way I could have done that without you."

"I know you couldn't have," Noah replied, punching Ben on the shoulder. "And it was disgusting. You owe me big."

Scout snorted and rolled around on the grass. He swatted at something in the air and tipped himself over by accident. Hero sniffed his way across the lawn, following the scent of a long-gone squirrel or chipmunk.

Something caught Ben's eye in the street. It was a black SUV with tinted windows, moving very slowly down the block. It stopped in front of his house. Ben felt like someone was looking at them, but he couldn't see inside.

"Who's that?" Noah asked.

"No idea," Ben said.

Before Ben had a chance to think much about the car, Scout jumped two feet straight up in the air and let out a loud yelp. Ben ran over to where Scout was staring intensely at the grass. A cricket hopped out, and Scout startled again.

"Shhhh, boy. It's just a bug. Sit." Scout sat down, then lay on his side. Ben gave him a tummy rub. "You know, for a dog, you're a real scaredy-cat, Scout." Ben looked up at Noah with a worried expression.

"Give him some time," Noah said, reading his mind.

Beyond him, Ben saw the SUV pulling away. He noticed that it had a dented back bumper. He turned his attention back to Noah.

"I know," Ben said, unconvinced.

"Okay, see you tomorrow," Noah said as he jumped onto his bike.

"See you tomorrow," Ben called after him.

Ben watched as Noah headed off down the street on his bike. He reached the end of the block and turned the corner. A moment later, the black SUV turned after him and disappeared.

7

"WATCH THIS ONE, NOAH!" BEN SHOUTED. "Hero, go."
Hero headed off down a row of cars, sniffing the ground
as he went.

It was the weekend, and Ben and Noah were working in the used car lot that Noah's dad owned. But Ben
wasn't doing what he was supposed to be doing. Instead
of picking up the trash that had collected in the scrap
yard, he was training Hero. He couldn't help himself.
It was just too cool to give Hero commands in a new
environment. Noah, on the other hand, was trying hard
to do his work, but Ben kept distracting him.

Ben held the broom in one hand and gave Hero a
hand signal with the other.

"Okay, Hero," Ben called out. "Stop!" Hero stopped instantly and turned his gaze to Ben. Without a word, Ben held his hand out to his side and gave Hero the hand signal for *come*. Hero dashed back to Ben's side.

"Good boy!" Ben praised him.

"Nice," Noah said.

"Maybe Scout will be able to do all this one day," Ben said. At the sound of his name, Scout bounced over to Ben. He sat down at Ben's feet, next to Hero, and looked up at him, his eyes round with anticipation. "You're looking for a treat, huh, Scout?" Ben laughed. "You have to earn it! You can't just get it for being cute."

Customers wandered around the lot, poking their noses into the different cars, kicking the tires as if that would tell them anything useful. On the far side of the lot, Noah's dad stood talking to a woman next to a gleaming sports car. Ben, Noah, and the dogs were in a quiet area off to the side, where some cars were dismantled for parts. There was a row of metal shelving units lined with carburetors and bumpers and other various spare parts from what seemed like every car ever driven.

Hero's thick coat glistened in the early spring sunlight

as he waited patiently for his next command. Scout, on the other hand, wriggled and whined excitedly. His soft, fuzzy fur was covered in dust.

"Okay, Scout, time to learn from the master. Watch this, okay?"

Ben snatched Noah's baseball cap from his head. Noah tried to grab it back but wasn't fast enough. "Hey," he groaned, rubbing his matted blond hair.

Ben held the hat under Hero's nose. "Hero, sniff."

Hero gave the hat a series of quick little snorts. Ben knew from his reading that Hero could smell tens of thousands of times better than any human. Hero was sorting out all the different odors on the hat and, in a way, committing them to memory. He was also prioritizing them—Noah's scent would be the strongest. A trained rescue dog like Hero would be able to track the hat—or a person, or whatever it was they needed him to track—for miles and days, just from smelling an object with the matching scent on it.

"Hero, stay." Ben gave him the hand signal and stepped away. Hero stayed put. He let out one short whimper, excited to start the game.

"I feel you, Hero," Noah said, rolling his eyes. "But you know how Ben gets."

"Very funny, you two," Ben shot back over his shoulder. He walked down a row of mismatched cars in varying states of repair, then turned left near a huge pickup truck. Ben was out of Hero's sight now. He walked several cars farther and stashed the cap on the ground beneath a minivan.

As he walked back toward the dogs, Ben noticed that Scout had started to put on a little weight. It had been only a few days since he and Hero had found him, but already the pup looked much healthier. Ben felt relieved that they'd found Scout when they did.

"You watching?" Ben asked. Noah nodded. Scout yipped. "Hero, search!"

Hero was off like a shot, racing down the long row of cars and disappearing around the corner. He was back in seconds, Noah's cap dangling from his mouth.

"Attaboy, Hero!" Ben gave the dog a treat. Hero kicked up dust with his tail. "Drop it, Hero," Ben said. Hero released Noah's cap onto the ground. Ben picked it up and handed it back to his friend.

Noah grimaced and tried to wipe off the slobber and dirt that had collected on the brim, then gave up and put it back on his head. "Impressive," Noah said. "I guess it's Hero's lucky hat too."

"That's nothing for Hero," Ben said, grinning. "That's like a warm-up exercise for him."

Scout started yipping like crazy. He ran in a wide circle around Hero, his tongue hanging out of his mouth, his ears flapping in the breeze as he moved. He barked playfully at Hero until Hero hopped up and chased the puppy. His tail sticking straight up in the air, Scout bolted off as fast as he could—which was pretty fast, but not speedy enough to outrun Hero. Hero caught up to Scout, then passed him, and suddenly Scout was chasing Hero, his short legs pumping hard.

For the first time since Ben had found him, Scout looked happy and free, not anxious at all.

"Those are some great dogs you've got there," said a deep, scratchy voice behind him.

Ben and Noah spun around. A man stood behind them, squinting at Scout running in the distance. The man held a used rearview mirror in his hand, which he'd taken from the spare parts shelf. "The big one's got a good nose. And the puppy's quick."

Ben grinned with pride. "Thanks," he said. "Hero's a natural. And Scout—the puppy—is learning fast."

"Scout, huh?" the man said. "That what you call him?"

Ben nodded.

"I see," the man said simply. He was tall and thin, with piercing blue eyes. His face was lined with deep creases. He watched Scout prance back toward them.

"He sure does look familiar," the man said as he inched closer to Scout.

Before Ben had a chance to reply, Scout suddenly went berserk. He let out a loud and desperate wail and crouched down as low as he could, like he was trying to hide in plain sight. He barked fiercely and his whole body shook in terror.

"What's the matter, Scout?" Ben said, surprised. He dropped to his knees. "Whoa, buddy—" Ben reached out a hand to pet him, but the puppy scooted away from him. Hero zipped over to Scout's side and hovered over him protectively. Hero surveyed the lot, looking for whatever threat had upset the puppy. There was nothing there. No other animals. No loud noises.

"What's wrong with him?" Noah asked, concerned. "Did he hurt himself?"

"I have no idea," Ben said, panic starting to rise in his chest. One minute Scout was happy and running around, and the next he was a mess. It didn't make sense. He turned to ask the man if he had noticed anything. But the man was gone.

Ben turned back to Scout. The puppy had stopped shaking, and his body began to relax. Ben held out his hand again. This time, Scout sniffed it and let Ben touch his head. Ben ran his hand softly over Scout's back.

"It's okay, Scout. Shh . . ." Ben sat down on the ground. "He seems all right now," Ben said to Noah. He scooped up Scout and held him on his lap. The dog melted into Ben's chest. They sat like that, Hero leaning on Ben's leg, until Ben could feel Scout's heart rate slowing down.

"Maybe he's just tired." Noah squatted down next to them and put his hand on Scout's downy fur. Scout licked his fingers. "Right, Scout? You're just getting used to us and all these new sights and sounds."

"Yeah." Ben sighed. "You're probably right." The last few days had been a lot of excitement for such a little puppy. Especially for a puppy who had, at best, been left all alone with no food or anyone to take care of him—and at worst, treated like garbage. Either way it must have been pretty scary. Like his dad had said the day he'd brought Scout home, one bad experience could change a dog's life.

"Ben," Noah said, his voice a little tentative. "Um, not to change the subject or anything, but . . . It's great that you're so into Hero and Scout, but tryouts are really soon, remember? Don't you want to let the dogs rest for the day and go hit a few balls?"

Ben shook his head. "I'd love to, but I can't." Ben put Scout down on the ground and stood up. "He's so stressed out—I don't want to leave him alone."

Noah shot him a skeptical look. "Okay. Well, our shift is up, and since I did all your work for you, I'm gonna head home."

Ben looked sheepish. "Thanks. I owe you one."

"I don't think 'one' is the number you're looking for there, pal," Noah shot back with a grin. "But you're welcome."

Noah hopped on his bike and pedaled off. As he headed out through the gate, Ben's dad drove into the lot in his police car. Noah waved at him as he passed. Ben's dad parked and hopped out. He strode over to Ben in his full uniform. His boots were shined to a high gloss, and his wide leather belt was loaded with a variety of tools and gadgets. Ben was always amazed at how serious and impressive his dad looked in uniform. Hero ran over to his dad's side.

"Hey, boy!" Ben's dad gave the dog a good scratch under the collar. "Hey, Ben."

"Hi, Dad. What're you doing here?" Ben asked, surprised. His dad rarely left his shift to come say hello.

"I came to tell you some news. The first thing is, no one has reported a missing puppy. And I called around to the shelter and the vet, and no one seems to be looking for the little man."

Ben held his breath. Was his dad going to let him keep Scout?

"The other thing is that I talked to the guys at the vet who've been taking care of the injured strays we've been finding. Looks like Scout's wounds are definitely the same as on the dogs we believe came from the fighting racket. He's had it rough."

"So what do we do?" Ben asked.

"Well . . ." His dad exhaled slowly. "We can't just put him in the shelter after all he's been through. Your mom and I talked, and we've decided we can foster him until we decide whether or not he should stay or whether we need to find him a new home."

Ben wanted to let out a cheer but figured he'd better play it cool. He wanted his parents to think he was mature enough to handle two dogs after all. So he just nodded. "That's great. Thanks, Dad."

His dad gave him a look that said there was more

to the story. "But just because we *can* keep him doesn't mean we *should*," his dad went on. He put a hand on Ben's shoulder. "You need to be honest with us if you feel like you're overloaded."

"I promise." Ben nodded earnestly, but he couldn't stop himself from breaking into a huge grin. "I'll let you know. It'll be fine. I can handle it."

"Glad to hear it." His dad looked around the lot. "How's work going?"

Oh man—work. Ben hadn't picked up a single piece of trash. His dad read the look on his face and turned to Ben with an irritated expression. "Seriously, Ben? What've you been doing here all afternoon?"

"I'm sorry, Dad. I got distracted," Ben said quietly.

"By what?" His dad's voice was soft but stern.

Ben didn't know what to say. He didn't want to lie to his dad, but he didn't want to let him know that Scout was a distraction either. Both options ended with Scout going away. Before he could figure out what to say, his dad shook his head. "The dogs, right? You got distracted by the dogs?"

Ben nodded. "I was practicing some commands with Hero. And then Scout wanted to try, and . . ." Ben didn't bother finishing his sentence.

His dad pinched his lips together in a straight line. "You're on someone else's payroll here, Ben. You know that your mom and I are pretty lenient with the rules, but you have to prove to us that you deserve this."

"I know, Dad."

"Believe me, I understand better than anyone how amazing it is to work with a great dog"—his dad gestured to Hero—"but that is not your top priority right now, okay?" He studied his son's face for a moment. "Have your mom and I made a mistake here?"

"No!" Ben cried out, louder than he meant to. "I promise—I can handle it," he said in an upbeat voice.

"You really just seem to have too much on your plate, son. Maybe Scout is one thing too many."

Ben started to feel desperate. "I messed up today. But I can handle it, Dad. I swear. I'll try even harder. Hero is family, and Scout—I just—I don't know." He pictured Scout cowering in the woods again. "He's really special to me."

"I know, Ben." His dad looked up at the sky for a moment. He seemed to be weighing what to do next. Then he looked around. "Speaking of Scout, where is he?"

Ben scanned the lot. The puppy was nowhere to be seen.

"He was just right here." Ben felt his stomach clench. First Scout started barking uncontrollably, and next he's disappeared? Today was not going well.

Ben ran through the sea of cars, searching around and under each one. No Scout. Finally he looked behind the small building that served as the office. Scout was scrunched up against the back wall of the structure, doing his best to disappear completely. He was shaking again. Ben scooped him up and held him tight.

"Shhhhhh. It's okay, Scout." He carried the puppy around to the front, where his dad stood with Hero. At the sight of Ben's dad, Scout began barking and whining frantically, desperately. He scrambled to get out of Ben's arms, but Ben held on to him. "Hey—Scout, chill, pup. Take it easy!"

"Something's really gotten into him, huh?" Ben's dad said. "Was he fine before I showed up?" Ben's dad took a step backward, and Scout calmed down a little. Ben loosened his grip for a split second, and in that instant, Scout launched himself from Ben's arms. The pup landed on the ground and skittered away as fast as he could, weaving among the cars.

Ben felt like he'd been punched in the gut. Something wasn't right. It was like Scout had two parts to his personality—he was smart and sweet, but he was also incredibly skittish. If Ben couldn't fix Scout's anxiety problems, there was no way the pup could ever stay with his family. His parents would never allow it.

"Ben, I've seen what happens to these fighting dogs, and trust me, I can't unsee it," his dad said gently. "It's horrible. If Scout is going to get past what happened to him, he'll need someone to spend a lot of time with him—more time than you have on your hands."

Frustration rose in Ben's chest. There was no way his dad was taking away Scout. Ben couldn't find the words to explain to his dad how he felt about both of the dogs. He couldn't imagine life without Hero—it was almost like he was a part of Ben. And Scout was just so tiny and young . . . he needed Ben and Hero. Even in the few days since they'd found him, Ben felt like Scout had already come to rely on him. He couldn't just abandon him.

The only way to convince his dad, though, would be to prove him wrong. And that's just what Ben planned to do.

"I just—please, Dad?"

Ben's dad studied his son's face. He shook his head and looked away. Ben bit his lip to stop himself from begging. Finally, his dad spoke. "You're putting me in a tough spot here, Ben. I can see how much Scout means to you. But I can also tell that he's maybe not the best thing for you." He sighed. "One more chance. Please don't make me regret it."

8

"BEN, YOUR NEXT ASSIGNMENT IS TO interview our new student, uh . . ." Ms. Malik consulted an official-looking piece of paper on her desk. "Jack Murphy."

"What? No!" Ben called out before he could stop himself. "I mean, can't someone else do that?" He looked around the school newspaper office. All the other kids stared at their computer screens or, conveniently, seemed to be looking for something very important at the bottoms of their backpacks.

"You're it," Ms. Malik said firmly. "I'll need five hundred words on where he came from, what he likes to do in his spare time, sports, family. You know the drill. Let's get to know him."

"Yes, Ms. Malik." *Ugh*.

"He'll be here any minute."

Double ugh. Not only did Ben have to spend the rest of the period talking to Jack, of all people, but he'd hoped to spend some of Newspaper Club getting a head start on his homework. He was heading over to the police station after school. He wanted to take Hero back to say hello to everyone, and Ben was hoping to meet one of the K-9 officers his dad had been telling him about— Officer Perillo. He was hoping she might be able to give him some advice on helping Scout get over his nerves.

For a second, Ben entertained the possibility of faking a sudden-onset stomachache before Jack got there, but he knew he'd never get away with it.

"Great," Ben said to Ms. Malik, faking enthusiasm.

A few minutes later, Ben sat face-to-face with the kid who had tried to crack his skull open with a fastball. Jack looked about as happy to be there as Ben.

"So, you moved here from Jackson how long ago?" Ben asked.

"Three months," Jack said, fiddling with the Mississippi State University Bulldog key chain that hung off his backpack.

"And did you play any sports back in Jackson?" Ben

already knew the answer, but he had to ask the question.

"Baseball," Jack said quietly. He sure wasn't making this interview any easier for either one of them.

"Were you on the varsity team?" Ben asked, trying to sound like a real reporter and pull out the interesting details of Jack's life.

"Yep."

"What position did you play?" Ben tried again.

"Shortstop."

Ben's stomach tightened. It was true, then. Jack was going to be his competition for the spot. "And, uh, how did your team do?" Ben asked nervously.

Jack's face lit up. "You don't know?"

"Uh, nope. Sorry," Ben said.

"We swept the state, man." Jack grinned. "Number one, three years in a row. Way better than your team did, that's for sure."

"Three years, wow," Ben said through gritted teeth, trying hard to ignore the rest of the comment.

"When my mom said we were moving here, the first thing I did was look up your team," Jack said. "To make sure you don't suck. Turns out you don't, which is nice."

Ben tightened his grip on his pen. "Glad you approve," he said.

"Your team isn't up to the same level I'm used to," Jack said. "But that could change. Tryouts are in two days." As if Ben needed a reminder. "I heard you play shortstop too." Jack looked Ben up and down as he spoke.

Ben couldn't tell if Jack was messing with him or not. Either way, it was getting to him. Ben could feel his blood starting to boil. *Breathe,* he heard his dad's voice say. *Act with purpose.* Ben inhaled, exhaled. He just needed to get the assignment done.

"That's right. I do," Ben replied as neutrally as he could. "So," he said, changing the subject, "what was it that brought you and your family to Gulfport right in the middle of the semester?"

Ben saw a flicker of something—was it sadness?—cross Jack's face. When he spoke again, he sounded a little less confident.

"It's not my whole family," Jack said. "It's just me and my mom." He looked around the room. "My parents are getting divorced. My mom got a new job here, so we moved."

"Oh, uh . . . sorry," Ben said. "I didn't mean to . . ."

"It's cool," Jack said with a shrug. "I guess I'll see my dad every few months or something like that."

From what Ben could tell, there was nothing about the situation that could be defined as "cool." It had to be hard living in a new town and not seeing your dad for months at a time. Ben couldn't believe it, but he actually felt bad for Jack. He was fumbling for what to say next when someone tapped him on the shoulder. Noah had come into the room.

"What's going on, gentlemen?" he asked, looking from Ben to Jack and back again. His eyebrows were raised in surprise.

"Hey, Noah," Ben said. He shot his friend a look that said *Don't ask*.

"Uhhh . . . I just came to figure out the plan for Friday night," Noah said.

"Friday night?" It sounded vaguely familiar, but Ben couldn't put his finger on what he was talking about. He was aware of Jack listening to their conversation.

"My mom's surprise birthday party! Am I going to need to remind you again, or can you hang on to this info for three more days?"

"I'll remember," Ben said. Noah looked unconvinced.

"You have to let everyone into my house while we take her out for dinner."

"Right."

"Dude, if you're not there on time, the whole surprise will be ruined. My dad and I are counting on you."

"Gotcha." He gestured with his head toward Jack. "Uh, I'm almost done here, if you want to wait for me."

Noah checked the time on his phone.

"Can't. Gotta run to study group. Bye, Jack."

Jack nodded at him. Noah pinned his gaze on Ben again.

"Friday," he said.

"Friday," Ben repeated. "I'll be there."

"You'd better be. Or a jittery dog will be the least of your problems."

9

BEN HAD HIS STORY PREPARED. IF he ran into his dad at the police station, he'd just tell him that he'd brought Hero to see his old friends. Ben would leave out the part about finding Officer Perillo.

Thankfully, his dad was out on a call that afternoon, but the officer at the front desk had known Ben since he was little—and he definitely knew Hero. The older man waved them through to the squad room. Ben, Hero, and Scout wandered through the station looking for Officer Perillo. Every few feet, someone stopped them, shouting, "Hero!" Uniformed officers, administrative staff—even the police chief—all dropped to their knees to say hi to the dog. Hero's tail was going a mile a minute. Meanwhile, Scout cowered in Ben's arms, shaking with fear at all the commotion. Ben soothed him as best he could, but Scout's eyes flitted around the room nervously.

"So that's the pup your dad was talking about," said a young woman as she walked toward them. Ben nodded at the officer, who wore a uniform shirt with K-9 stitched on the front, just like his dad's. She held out her hand to shake. "I'm Janine Perillo. You must be Ben."

"Hi, nice to meet you," Ben said, trying to grip her hand as firmly as possible. "This is Scout. And you know Hero."

"Heeeeero!" Perillo wrapped her arms around Hero's neck. He licked her face and let out a happy whine.

"He likes you." Ben laughed.

"Hero and I had some fun together. He trained me," she said.

"Don't you mean you trained him?"

Perillo laughed as Hero nipped at her dark hair. "Nope. Compared to him, I'm the rookie around here. Hero taught me the ropes. Did your dad ever tell you about the bank robber?"

Ben shook his head. He held Scout tighter.

Perillo smiled as she called up the memory and gave

Hero a good scratch behind the ears. "It was my very first assignment. You can imagine how nervous I was. We were out searching for this guy who'd robbed a bunch of banks along the Mississippi coast. The guy had an invisibility cloak or something. After every robbery, he'd just disappear. No one could find him. Anyway, this guy had just hit Gulfport, but by the time we got to the bank, he was long gone. All we had was the note he'd handed the teller. There were no fingerprints on it, of course, because he'd worn gloves. But his scent was on it, and Hero here"—she paused to rub her nose on Hero's nose—"was like 'I got this.'

"Hero sniffed the paper, followed the robber's trail out of the bank. He led your dad and me into an office building, then down to the basement. I was a nervous wreck, because I had no idea what we were going to find. Sure enough, in the boiler room was the bank robber, just hanging out and counting his money. His whole trick was to hide nearby, because cops always assume a thief takes off and tries to get as far away as possible. Then when the coast was clear, he'd sneak out of town. That guy was not too happy about meeting Hero."

Perillo wrapped her arm around Hero's neck and pulled him close. "Hero taught me a lot that day, and he's the reason I joined the K-9 unit. He's the best there ever was. Right, buddy?" Hero dropped to the floor and rolled onto his back. She scratched his belly.

Ben got goose bumps just thinking about Hero on the job—he wished he'd gotten a chance to see his dog save lives and catch bad guys. "He's pretty special," Ben said. "And it turns out he's also kind of a softie."

"What do you mean?" Perillo asked. "Hero's tough as nails."

"He's both, I guess." Ben laughed as he set Scout down on the ground. The puppy jumped onto Hero's back and began gnawing on his black tail. "Hero is crazy for Scout here, but if you try to come between them, he'll stop you. It's like, I don't know, he's just super protective of Scout."

"Aw," Perillo said, grinning. "Hero, I didn't know you were the paternal type." Hero's tongue hung out of his mouth. He licked his chops and snapped his jaw shut. His ears perked up as he looked from Ben to Perillo and back.

"It's really sweet," Ben said, "but there's one problem. Scout is really scared all the time. And unless I can get him to calm down, my parents aren't going to let me keep him. Hero is not going to like that very much."

"No," Perillo said. "I imagine he wouldn't."

"Hero and I have been trying to train Scout, but I think we need some help. My dad said you're the best trainer on the force. I was hoping maybe you could give me some advice?"

"Sure," Perillo said. "I'd be happy to. Anything for Hero." She gave the puppy a soothing rub behind the ears. Scout looked back at her with a combination of suspicion and fear in his eyes.

"You're a scared one, huh," she said softly. "It's okay, Scout."

Ben couldn't believe it: Scout's little body relaxed. He wiggled off Hero's back and tentatively stuck out his nose, sniffing at the air around Perillo. After a moment, she held out her hand. Scout nudged it with his wet nose, then let the officer pet his head.

"Wow," Ben said. He crouched down next to them.

"Dogs like me. What can I say?" Perillo shrugged. "Have you seen our new training course?"

"No, can I?" Ben asked. "My dad said it's pretty cool!"

Behind the police station was, indeed, the coolest thing Ben had ever seen. It was somewhere between a massive obstacle course and a disaster scene, formed by a landscape of wrecked cars, slatted wooden pallets, giant concrete pipes to crawl through, and crumbling concrete slabs. At the far end of the course was a tall structure that looked like a tree house, with a ladder leading up to a landing.

Ben watched as a beautiful caramel-and-white Akita ran across a rickety pallet propped up at an angle. Her trainer stood off to the side, watching the dog move carefully but quickly, skidding through a pipe, and hop out on the other side. The dog climbed up the rear bumper of an overturned car. She slid down the windshield, nosed her way around a pile of concrete blocks, and barked three times—her signal that she'd found something.

"Good girl, Mocha!" her trainer called out. "Come!"

"Wow . . ." Ben said.

"Pretty cool, huh? We didn't have this when Hero was in training," Perillo said. "But it's amazing what the dogs can do in there. It's an agility course, but it's built to simulate real disaster conditions. We need to prepare the dogs for whatever they might encounter out there in the field. There are even loudspeakers and bright lights we can use. It's the best way to train them to tune out distractions, like thunder or lightning or gunfire. That way we teach the dogs to be totally focused on saving lives."

While Perillo talked, Hero gazed longingly at the training course and wagged his tail. Ben and Perillo laughed and shared a look.

"Can Hero . . . ?" Ben asked with a nod toward the course.

"Of course," Perillo said with a wink. "Hero, go!" She gave the command.

Hero took off like a shot. Ben was in awe as Hero made his way quickly to the top of an overturned police van, jumped onto a massive concrete block, then moved with incredible precision across a haphazard, wobbly stack of pallets. He turned a sharp corner and went over an A-frame ramp. All the while, Hero sniffed everything around him, processing the thousands of scents that drifted on the air and rested on every surface.

All the other trainers stopped their work to watch Hero go.

He stepped through a gravel pit and headed toward the ladder leading up to the tree house. Hero launched himself onto the bottom rung and shimmied up the ladder with ease.

Ben gasped. He didn't know dogs could climb

ladders. It was amazing to watch. On the landing above, Hero suddenly stopped and sat down. That was what he'd been trained to do when he'd located a "find"—in this case, a dummy that had been placed there by a trainer. Everyone cheered for Hero.

"He's still the fastest dog around," Perillo said. "What a champ!"

Hero made his way back down and trotted over to Ben, Scout, and Perillo. He was barely even panting. Ben gave him a treat.

"Good job, Hero!" he said.

"He's magic," Perillo said, shaking her head in amazement. Scout bounded over to Hero like he wanted to play too. Perillo studied Scout. "I think the first thing Scout needs to do is build his confidence. What do you say, Scout? You wanna give it a try?"

Scout blinked at her, then looked up at Ben.

"Isn't he a little young?" Ben asked.

"He's too little to climb up the cars or the ladder, but he can handle a lot of it," Perillo said.

Ben was nervous. Was Scout going to freak out? He walked Scout over to the edge of the course.

"Scout, go!" Ben said. Scout whined and did a nervous little dance with his front paws. Hero sat by the sidelines, waiting patiently. Ben could tell that Scout wanted to do it. But he was afraid. "It's okay, Scout. Go!"

Scout put one paw on a concrete block.

"Speak from here," Perillo said to Ben, putting her hand on her stomach. "You're not asking him; you're telling him. Your tone needs to let him know you're in charge."

Ben tried it again. "Scout, go!" he said, projecting his voice. He heard the difference right away—his tone was fuller and more authoritative.

Scout stepped onto the rubble and made his way forward.

"There you go," Perillo said. "You spoke with conviction. And see—Scout heard it too. It'll make him feel more secure to know you're really in charge. You're his pack leader."

Scout scurried up a ramp, picking up speed and wagging his tail. He stopped at the top and looked down at the ground, clearly excited by the new perspective on things—but maybe a little unsure of how to get down. He hesitated for a moment, then stuck one paw out. Scout was leaning down at a sharp angle, and he didn't seem to like it very much. He quickly pulled his paw back up.

"Good boy, Scout," Ben said, trying to infuse his voice with positive—but firm—reinforcement. But Scout was stuck. He was too scared to move forward, and had no idea how to get back. The puppy started to shake and let out a sad, frightened howl. Hero bolted onto the course, clambered up the ramp, and stopped right behind Scout. Hero nudged at Scout's rump, trying to get him to move forward, but Scout was paralyzed with fear. Hero nudged him again, harder this time, and showed Scout the route to get down. Nothing seemed to reassure the puppy.

Finally, after a few minutes, Hero picked up Scout by the scruff—gently gripping the skin on the back of the puppy's neck with his mouth, like a mother dog does to her babies. Scout went slack in Hero's jaws. Hero carried him across the field of rubble and back to Ben and Perillo. He gently placed the puppy on the ground and licked him a few times. Scout's ears hung low and his tail was between his legs. He looked miserable.

Ben felt hopeless. "Is there anything I can do to help Scout?" he asked, trying not to sound too desperate.

Perillo considered his question carefully. "He's really nervous, for sure," she said. "But don't give up on him, Ben. He's still young, and he's only been with you for a little bit. You'll just have to wait and see if a safe environment and regular training are enough to soothe his nerves."

"So what should I do?" Ben asked.

"Keep working with him. Show him lots of love, but be the alpha dog too. Be consistent and positive, but assertive. Check in with me in a couple of weeks, and we'll see how far he's come."

"Thank you so much, Officer Perillo," Ben said.

Scout was just starting to relax again when a police siren roared to life in the nearby parking lot. Tires screeched as the car peeled out. Scout jumped up and scurried back toward the obstacle course. He wormed his way into a small space under a stack of pallets and hid in the darkness, shaking with fear.

"Scout, no!" Ben called out. "Scout, come!" Scout stayed where he was, his ears flattened against his head and his eyes big and round. Ben was crushed. He looked at Perillo. She was shaking her head.

"Good luck, Ben," she said, sounding almost apologetic. "He's a great pup, but he's had a rough go of it."

10

BEN, HERO, AND SCOUT HEADED OUT to the parking lot. It had taken Hero and Ben a while to coax Scout out from under the pallets, but the puppy had finally calmed down. Ben looped Hero's leash around the bike rack while he unclipped Scout's leash. He started to tuck Scout into the carrier strapped to the back of his bike.

Just then, the engine of a police cruiser started up a few feet away. The car pulled out into the street, and the sound of its siren cut through the air like an explosion. Ben's eardrums vibrated. Hero didn't even flinch—he sat calmly next to Ben—but Scout's whole body stiffened. Before Ben had time to react, the puppy had jumped out of the carrier, landed on the asphalt, and taken off.

Scout moved so fast across the parking lot and toward the road that he was a blur. Hero, who was held back by his leash, barked frantically after Scout.

"Scout, stop!" Ben yelled. "Scout, stay!"

In the blink of an eye, Scout turned onto the sidewalk outside the station and was gone.

"Hero, go!" Ben cried out, unclipping Hero's leash from his harness. "You're going to have to figure out where he went, okay?" he said. "Hero, find Scout."

Hero skimmed his nose across the sidewalk, his head moving rapidly back and forth as he followed Scout's scent. He looked up for a second, turned back to Ben, then took off running down the street. Ben pedaled as fast as he could to keep up. Hero was in full tracking mode. His body moved in a perfect, beautiful stride, like an elegant machine.

Ben wasn't familiar with the area around the police station. Hero zigzagged through the neighborhood and led Ben to the beachside road that ran for miles along the Gulf of Mexico. Ben hardly noticed the endless stretch of white-sand beaches. Hero and Ben turned inland and headed down the quiet, residential streets, where porches wrapped around old mansions, and quite a few houses had tall columns out front. They skirted the airport and trudged along the sludgy banks of a bayou.

Soon they were miles away. Ben began to doubt Hero. Surely Scout couldn't have run this far? Finally, as the sky was starting to dim to a dull gray, Hero slowed his pace. They were on the outskirts of town, in a neighborhood Ben had never been to before. It was a desolate stretch—not quite residential, not quite rural. There were big patches of land between the houses, some with overgrown grass and tall weeds.

No one was out walking. There were no kids playing in front yards. It was quiet and isolated. Ben couldn't picture sweet, innocent Scout in a creepy neighborhood like this. It made him feel queasy just thinking about it.

They turned a corner, and Hero started barking and picking up speed again. He bolted toward the last house on the block, sat down in the driveway, and waited for Ben to catch up. Huffing and puffing, Ben pulled up next to Hero and gave the dog a treat.

He caught his breath and looked over the house. It was newish and simple, nothing fancy. One-story, red-brick, with a driveway running up the side. When Ben saw what was parked in that driveway, a weird feeling washed over him. It was a black SUV.

For a split second, Ben couldn't place the car—or

put his finger on why it was making the hair on the back of his neck stand up. Then, suddenly, it clicked: It was the same truck he'd seen driving slowly by his house last week, when he was on the lawn with Noah. He recognized the dented bumper.

A brown-and-white ball of movement barreled down the driveway and jumped up on Ben's legs. Scout! The puppy barked and wagged his tail so hard it almost spun his tiny body in circles. Ben was flooded with relief. He leaned over to pick up the puppy, and Scout wiggled in his arms and licked his face.

"I'm happy to see you too, Scout! You scared the heck out of me." Ben looked down at Hero. "Nice work, Hero." Hero just panted in response. He didn't need thanks; he'd done exactly what he was trained to do.

At the sound of a door slamming shut, Ben looked up at the house. A tall, thin man was making his way down the driveway. Every muscle in Hero's body tensed as his protective instincts kicked in. Scout trembled in Ben's arms and burrowed himself into Ben's sweatshirt.

As the man got closer, Ben realized he'd seen him before—it was the same guy he'd talked to at the car lot. The one who had complimented his dogs.

The man stopped a few feet away.

"I know you, kid," the man said.

Ben nodded but didn't respond. The man looked Hero up and down, then locked his gaze on the puppy. "Scout, right?" His tone was different today. He didn't sound as friendly as he had before.

"Yeah, Scout," Ben said. This guy gave him the creeps. "Uh, thanks, sir. We just came to get the puppy. We'll get off your property now."

The man let out a hoarse laugh. "I'm no 'sir.' You can call me Mitch." The man's mouth moved into something resembling a smile. "What's the rush?"

Ben didn't like the look in Mitch's eye. It was cold— like his mouth and his eyes were feeling two totally different things.

"You ever think of fighting these dogs?" Mitch asked, the fake smile still on his face.

"Fighting them? What do you mean—" Ben stopped mid-sentence. Dogfighting. Ben shuddered. "No, sir. No way. Hero is a police dog. And Scout here is just a puppy."

The man nodded but said nothing. His eyes flashed up to Ben's face. Ben held his gaze for as long as he could, finally looking away.

"We're gonna go," Ben said firmly. "Hero, come."

Hero hopped up and stood by Ben's side as he got on his bike.

Without a word, Mitch turned and headed back into his house, slamming the screen door behind him. Ben exhaled and hustled the dogs away from the house as fast as he could.

As he biked home, Ben's mind raced, trying to process the long chase and the weird dude at the house. Mitch. Everything about that guy had made Ben feel uneasy—the things he said, the way he looked at Hero and Scout, the way he acted like Ben hardly even existed.

By the time he pedaled up his driveway, Ben was exhausted, and he could see that Hero and Scout were wiped out from the long day too. Ben gave them extra water and food and put Scout in his crate, making sure the latch was secure. Hero stayed downstairs, curled up on the floor next to Scout's crate. The two dogs, one big and one little, pressed against each other, separated only by the thin metal.

Just the sight of his dogs flooded Ben with a deep sense of appreciation and love. Hero had really come through for them that day, tracking Scout so far away. And Scout had seemed so relieved when they finally found him.

Scout was already sound asleep.

Hero looked around the room, inspecting it one last time before going to sleep. He spotted Ben watching him.

"Good night, buddy," Ben said from the stairs. Hero exhaled sharply through his nose, almost like a sigh, and shut his eyes.

11

"EVERYBODY UP," COACH LEE CALLED OUT. "Let's do some laps."

The boys ran in formation around the field. Ben didn't look up as he passed the crowded bleachers, but he knew his parents and Erin were there with Hero and Scout, ready to cheer him on for varsity tryouts.

Ben tried to focus on what he needed to accomplish. He needed to do everything right—there was no room for mistakes. He had to hit, field, and throw better than he ever had. He needed to make shortstop. Ben spotted Noah a few kids away. They gave each other an encouraging nod.

Coach Lee split them up for batting warm-ups. The

boys swung bats at invisible pitches, loosening up their arms. As Ben rotated his upper body, his arms and hands moving with perfect follow-through, his wrist rolling over at the end of his swing, he began to relax.

"Landry," Coach Lee called out. "You're up first."

Tryouts flew by. Ben hit two doubles. He connected with a fastball and a curveball. He tried not to get too excited about how well he was doing—he just stayed focused. When all the boys did sprints, Ben was at the head of the pack. Going into the fielding exercises, he felt strong and in the zone. But he didn't want to get ahead of himself.

The coach shouted out the boys' names and assigned them to various positions in the field. "Landry— shortstop!" Ben hustled over to his spot and surveyed the other players in the infield. Jack was at first base. Ben hadn't seen him since the other day, when Jack had told him about his parents' divorce. They caught each other's eye. Ben nodded, but Jack turned away without responding. Ben still didn't know what to make of the kid, but he couldn't think about that now. The last thing Ben needed was to get distracted.

The kids moved through a series of plays. Every fifteen minutes or so, Coach rotated the boys' positions—everyone except Ben and Jack. As the boys warmed up, the scrimmage picked up speed and intensity. Ben felt good. He caught every ball fired at him. He threw with precision and speed. He was totally focused on the ball, the other players, and the sound of his own breathing. He felt himself playing almost . . . instinctually. Like his body and mind were in perfect sync. Somewhere on the edges of his awareness, he could hear his family cheering him on.

There was a pause between plays while Coach Lee talked to one of the other players. Ben spotted Noah in the outfield and gave him a quick wave. Then someone shouted his name from the infield: "Landry!" Ben turned just in time to see Jack's arm unfurling in his direction, releasing a fastball. Ben's mind and body worked at warp speed. His reflexes kicked in, and he held up his mitt while ducking as fast as he could.

It wasn't fast enough.

The ball nailed him on his right collarbone, hard. The pain shot through his body. Ben doubled over and took short, sharp breaths, hoping he didn't pass out right there in the field. He could feel Jack's eyes on him. In the distance, Ben heard Hero barking angrily, and Noah yelling, "Hey!" Out of the corner of his eye, Ben saw Hero streaking around the chain-link fence and onto the field. He heard his dad yelling, "Hero, no!" But the dog was barking and growling viciously—he was trained to protect his handler at all costs—and he was heading straight for Jack. Jack cowered on first base, holding up his hands in front of him to ward off Hero.

Ben straightened up as quickly as he could. He cringed at the throbbing in his shoulder. He could barely catch his breath.

"Hero, no!" he called out weakly. But it was loud enough for Hero to hear, which was all that mattered. Hero practically froze just a few feet from Jack. Jack flinched.

Ben's dad ran out from the bleachers, calling out commands to Hero. He grabbed Hero's leash. Ben's dad caught his eye and mouthed the words *You okay?* to him. Ben nodded and gave his dad a thumbs-up with his good arm. With a worried look, his dad gave him a return thumbs-up and led Hero back to the benches.

Coach Lee jogged over to Ben.

"You okay, Landry?" Coach Lee asked in a worried tone.

"I'm good, Coach." Ben grimaced and rubbed his shoulder.

"I didn't see what happened, but I heard your dog. And the other guys said Jack fired a fastball at you. Is that right?" Coach Lee adjusted his baseball cap and gave Ben a serious look.

Ben didn't know what to say. His chest was killing him, and it sure seemed like Jack had tried to hurt him for no good reason. But he didn't want to rat out another kid. Coach talked to the team all the time about the importance of sportsmanship and keeping their tempers under control. He always told the boys, "Respect your opponents, respect your teammates, respect yourself."

"I'll take your silence as a yes." Coach headed over to Jack and said a few stern words. Jack stomped off the field, casting a nasty look back at Ben as he went.

Ben could see his family and the other parents talking to one another about what had just happened and pointing at him and Jack. The other players in the field were talking about it too.

"All right, guys," Coach Lee called out. "Let's focus. Everyone on the field, come in. You're up again."

The adrenaline shooting through Ben's body began to subside. His shock and confusion faded, though his shoulder continued to throb. Somehow he was able to regain his focus. He hit a triple and a straight shot into center field, which the center fielder caught. But still, Ben knew he was hitting his best. When he went back out into the field, he landed every throw.

An hour later, tryouts were over. Ben was exhausted but pumped. Whether he made first string or not, he knew he'd played his best. Despite Jack.

"Landry," Coach called out. Ben walked over to him. "Nice job today, Ben."

"Thanks, Coach."

"You're gonna do a great job at shortstop this year, kid." Coach clapped Ben on the back. Ben tried not to wince from the pain in his collarbone. "Congratulations."

Ben grinned. "Really?"

"Really. You worked hard for this. I can tell. Now get out of here and put some ice on that shoulder. I'm going to need you in top form for our first practice in two weeks."

Ben practically floated over to the dugout. He heard Coach's words over and over in his head. *You're gonna do a great job at shortstop . . . congratulations.* Ben was changing out of his cleats when Jack stormed by him in the dugout. His face was red.

"If it weren't for your dog, I would have made the team," Jack said.

Ben's mouth hung open. Did Jack seriously think Hero was the problem here? He was the one who threw a fastball at Ben!

Before Ben could think of a response, Jack strode off, still in his cleats. His mitt was tucked under his arm, and his fists hung clenched at his sides.

12

THE NEXT DAY AFTER SCHOOL, BEN spent the afternoon hauling junk out of the garage. He had a plan. A vision.

It was Friday, tryouts were over, and he was all caught up on his homework, at last. Ben was looking forward to spending the weekend with his dogs and this . . . contraption.

Ben stood back to admire his handiwork, hands resting on his hips. It wasn't pretty, but it should work. He had built a training course for Hero—a homemade version of the one at the police station. He had seen the joy in Hero's eyes when he was on the course, and it had occurred to Ben that maybe Hero missed his old life.

Ben knew that the best police dogs have a drive that

can't be taught. They're born to be trackers and rescuers. Ben didn't want Hero to get bored by civilian life—Hero deserved to be happy, even if that meant turning their backyard into a ridiculous-looking doggie amusement park. He was sure that his parents would understand. . . .

The first section of the course was a plastic tube from his sister's waterslide. Hero would have to run through it. Next was an A-frame ramp made from two boards leaning against a stack of old file boxes from the garage. Then there was a pile of loose gravel that Ben had poured on the grass. From there, Hero would jump up onto a narrow bridge made out of a long, skinny piece of plywood and four overturned buckets. He would run across the beam and jump down onto a bouncy air mattress. Then he would have to wade through a kiddie pool full of water. After that, Ben would towel him off and give him a treat.

Ben was also hoping that he and Hero could convince Scout to try the course. He was pushing Scout hard, he knew. But this could be just what Scout needed to overcome his nerves.

Hero loved the training course. He shimmied right through the plastic tube, scrambled up the ramp and slid down the other side, and happily tromped through the gravel. He practically flew over the beam like a trained gymnast. He danced across the air mattress, bobbing and weaving as the surface moved underneath him, then flung himself into the water with a giant splash. When he was done, he ran back to the beginning, his tail wagging like crazy. Ben gave him a scratch behind the ears and a treat while he dried him off.

Scout's first trip through the homemade course, however, was a disaster. He wouldn't set one paw into the tube. Hero had to go in after him and push him through to the other side. Scout climbed up the first half of the ramp, plopped onto his belly at the top, and rested his head on his paws. Hero had to nudge him up and over that too.

When Scout got to the gravel, he put one paw down and instantly jumped backward, yelping. Ben squatted down and scratched Scout under the chin. Hero walked back and forth across the gravel pile, showing Scout that there was nothing to be afraid of.

"It's okay, buddy. It's just rocks," Ben said. He scooped up a few and let them pour slowly from his palm. The loose stones clattered back onto the pile. Scout stepped forward and sniffed at them. "Scout, go,"

Ben said, using the hand signal. Scout took one tentative step as the rocks slipped and shifted beneath him. He took another step. Slowly he made his way forward, finally leaping up onto the wooden bridge. He pranced across it quickly, Hero running by his side.

"Attaboy," Ben encouraged him. "Scout, jump." Gaining courage, Scout jumped, caught a little air, and landed on the air mattress. He immediately bounced onto his back, all four paws in the air. "Come on, Scout. Up!" Ben said, motioning with his hand. With some effort, Scout rolled back onto his stomach and got up. He made his way slowly and carefully across as Hero and Ben walked alongside. When Scout got to the end of the mattress, he spied the water in the small plastic pool. Without hesitation, Scout jumped into it with a splash.

"Yes!" Ben pumped both arms into the air in triumph. Scout hopped out of the pool and shook off the water, showering Ben and Hero with droplets. "Good job, Scout!" Ben said, toweling off the puppy and giving him a treat. Hero let out a few happy barks and lapped up some pool water. Ben was so proud of Scout that he picked him up and squeezed him in a hug. Scout licked Ben's face and wagged his tail.

The dogs took turns going through the course until it was starting to get dark. Ben decided it was time to implement stage two. He wanted to keep Hero's training as real as possible, and it was pretty clear—after Scout's reaction to the police sirens—that the puppy needed to work on keeping his cool under pressure. Ben had scavenged a scrap of sheet metal from the garage. He was going to hold it up in the air and shake it to make a really loud noise while the dogs ran the course.

Ben bent over to pick up the metal from the ground. As he did, his phone fell out of his back pocket and landed on the grass. It flashed with six missed calls. All from Noah. Why had he called so many times? Something nagged at Ben—a funny feeling in the back of his brain that he'd forgotten something.

Ben called Noah back.

"Dude!" he said excitedly into the phone. "You'll never believe what the dogs are do—"

Noah cut him off. "Ben, where are you?" He was yelling. "I've been calling you for two hours."

"What are you talking ab—"

"My mother's surprise party? You were supposed to be here over an hour ago to let everyone in. Remember?" Noah's voice was filled with anger.

A wave of guilt and regret washed over Ben. He felt awful. "Noah, I'm so sorry—I totally forgot. I—"

"Everyone was just standing on the front lawn when we pulled up with my mom. You were supposed to let them inside so they could set up the party. But nothing was ready! Seriously lame, Ben."

"Noah, I'm so sorry, dude—" Ben began, but Noah had already hung up on him.

Ben put his face in his hands. It was like he couldn't do anything right. Or he could do one thing right, but only if he messed up five other things he was supposed to be doing at the same time.

"Hero! Scout! Come," Ben called out. Both dogs ran over to him and stood by his side. "Sorry, guys, but I have to go. Scout, in your crate." Ben moved Scout's cage onto the back patio. It would be too cold for the puppy to sleep out there, but he'd be okay for a couple of hours. Ben closed the small metal door and made sure to secure the latch.

Ben looked around and spotted a long rope looped around a tree in the backyard. When Hero had first come to live with them, Ben's parents had tied him to the tree during the day so he wouldn't wander over to Ben's school on his own. They hadn't used it in a while, but it was just what Ben needed right now. He tied the rope to Hero's harness.

"Keep Scout company, okay, Hero?" With a little grunt, Hero lay down near the crate. "I'll be back soon, guys," Ben said.

13

BEN HOPPED ON HIS BIKE AND headed down his driveway at top speed. He spotted a familiar person standing on the sidewalk outside his house and almost swerved into a tree. Jack.

Ben skidded to a stop. He and Jack locked eyes for a second, then Jack took off running down the block.

What was he doing at Ben's house? Jack lived a good half mile away—there was no reason for him to be at Ben's unless he was there on purpose. Ben's chest was still sore from Jack's fastball, and it wasn't like Jack had made any effort to apologize. But Ben didn't have time to wonder what he was up to. He had to get to Noah's and apologize.

He cursed himself all the way to Noah's house. He ran inside. Surf music poured through the living room speakers, and the air smelled distinctly of coconut. Ben remembered that it was a beach-vacation theme party, which for some reason just made him feel worse. Noah and his dad had put so much thought into planning the night, and he had messed it all up.

He waded through a crowd of dancing grown-ups, looking for Noah. He found him in the backyard, sitting on a deck chair and drinking a smoothie with a little paper umbrella in it.

"Noah," he said nervously. Noah turned around to look at him, then turned away.

"Go away," Noah said.

"I'm so sorry, man. I really messed up."

"Yeah," Noah said, still not looking at him. "You did."

Ben just stood there. He didn't know what else to say. After a long, silent moment, he said, "I'm gonna go find your parents and apologize." He turned to leave, but Noah spoke.

"You know, Ben, I'm always helping you out when you need me. In the last week alone I cleaned up your dog's mess with you and did your job when you were distracted. And you can't even do this one thing."

Ben felt so bad it was almost like a physical pain. There was no excuse—it was purely selfish to focus on Hero and Scout and forget about the promise he had made to his best friend. But it made him sick to think that Noah would ever feel like he was a bad friend.

"It's not an excuse, Noah, but I'm just—I'm just kind of . . . I don't know. Distracted. Right now, I mean—I guess I have a lot on my mind."

Noah sighed and finally looked at Ben. "You mean the dogs?"

"Yeah, partly. And baseball. And . . . I don't know. I just messed up. But it won't happen again, okay?"

Noah rolled his eyes at Ben. "You can bet that puppy it won't."

It was late by the time Ben got home from the party. He'd hung around for a while, hoping Noah would talk to him some more, but he hadn't. The night had pretty much sucked from beginning to end. Noah's parents had forgiven him, but that hadn't made Ben feel any better. He was just glad it was over and he was home again with his dogs. Ben headed around to the backyard to bring Scout in for the night.

It took a second for Ben to process what he was seeing. The crate was in the exact same spot, but the door was wide open. And it was empty. He looked around the yard, but Scout wasn't there. Hero was gone too.

Ben ran into the house. His parents had just gotten home from the movies with Erin. His mom was putting Erin to bed, but his dad was sitting at the kitchen table. Something on his dad's face told Ben he had been waiting for him.

"Hey, Dad," Ben said, trying not to seem anxious. He scanned the kitchen and living room for the dogs but didn't see them. Maybe his dad had let them go upstairs.

"Hey, son." Dave's gaze moved past Ben, as if he was looking for someone behind him. "No dogs?"

Ben was gripped by fear. His dad hadn't brought them inside. Both dogs were gone.

His dad was staring at him, like he was waiting for Ben to say something.

"No, they're at Noah's," Ben said, exhaling. He couldn't tell his dad the truth just yet—not until he knew where his dogs were. "You got my text that I was at Noah's mom's party, right?" Ben asked.

"I did."

"Good. The party was crazy—there were, like, four hundred coconuts at their house," Ben said, changing the subject so his dad wouldn't have time to wonder why he had taken the dogs to a party . . . and left them there. Before his dad had a chance to respond, Ben forced himself to yawn. "Well, I'm beat. I'm just gonna go to bed." He tried to move past his dad toward the stairs.

"I know you're tired, son, but let's talk for a sec, okay?" His dad's voice was firm. He gestured toward the seat next to him.

Ben's mouth went dry. He was in trouble for something, that much was clear. Normally the tone in his dad's voice would have been enough to freak him out. But now all he cared about was finding Scout and Hero. Ben bit his lip and focused on remaining calm. The last thing he needed was for his dad to know both dogs were missing. If he couldn't even keep them safe, there was no way his parents would let Ben keep them.

"Look, Ben." His dad sighed. "I don't want to start sounding like a broken record, but we need to talk about what's on your plate."

Ben nodded and squirmed a little in his chair. He forced himself to watch his dad's lips so he could absorb his words. Otherwise, his mind would wander in a thousand different directions as he tried to figure out what could possibly have happened to the dogs.

"Your mom and I thought you were doing better, but the school called me this afternoon. Seems you've been late almost every day for the last two weeks."

Ben cringed inside but tried not to let his panic show on his face.

"You're going to be thirteen in a few months," his dad started. "We've talked about this. Your mom and I really believe it's time for you to start acting with purpose. And we feel you're ready for some real responsibility, like the dogs. But I don't know—" His dad looked down and shook his head. "Maybe we let you take on too much all at once."

As if from a distance, Ben heard his dad say, "You're grounded, son," but it was the next words that sent a chill through him. "And the puppy has to go."

"No!" Ben shouted, before he could stop himself. His dad looked startled. "I mean—sorry, Dad, I didn't mean to yell. I'm just . . . upset. With myself," he added quickly. "I know I need to do better. I know I can do better." Suddenly he saw a way to buy himself some time, not to mention a little goodwill from his dad. "I mean, I knew I wasn't keeping up my end of the deal. That's why I took the dogs over to Noah's house. So I could study."

His dad sat back in his chair and studied Ben's face. He didn't say anything for a moment. Ben started to sweat, worried that his dad knew he was lying. Normally he'd never lie to either of his parents. Not only had he been brought up to believe lying to them was wrong, but, generally speaking, when your dad was a cop, it was better to tell the truth and take your licks. But this was not a normal situation. Ben had lost track of not one dog but two. As soon as he made sure Hero and Scout were safe, he'd tell his dad the truth and apologize for the whole mess.

"That's good to hear," his dad finally said. "I'm proud of you, Ben. You recognized the problem, and you worked out a solution." Ben instantly felt even worse. Now he was getting praise for something he didn't do. "You're still grounded for now, but stop giving the school reasons to call me, and I'll see what we can do about the puppy."

"Thank you, Dad. I'll get it together, I promise."

"Go on, then." His dad jerked a thumb toward the stairs.

Ben raced upstairs to his room, on the off chance that either of the dogs might be hiding in there.

It was empty.

He peeked in other rooms and in every closet and bathroom. No dogs. He even looked under his parents' bed, hoping against all reason that they would be snuggled together in the darkness.

Nothing. No Hero. No Scout.

Both of his dogs were gone.

14

BEN LAY ON HIS BED, EYES wide open. His room was dark.
He had turned off the light so his parents would think
he had gone to bed, but he was just waiting for them
to go to sleep so he could sneak out to find the dogs.
An electric current of fear wound its way through his
body. His throat felt tight, and he could feel his temples
pulsing.

Ben tried not to think about something horrible happening to Hero or Scout. He would never forgive himself. He needed help figuring out what to do next. He
needed Noah, but he had never seen his friend as mad as
he was earlier. It hardly seemed likely he'd be interested
in speaking to Ben right now, let alone helping him.

He'd have to do this on his own. After what felt like forever, the house was quiet, and the lights were out in every house on the block. Ben let himself out through the back door. He rode through the dark streets, softly calling for Hero and Scout. He felt like he was shouting in the deep silence.

Nothing. He rode through his entire neighborhood. He rode through the downtown shopping area, where gates covered the storefronts and parking lots stood empty. He rode along the beach, which was all shadows and creepiness in the middle of the night. Finally, when he thought he was going to have to give up, he rode over to Noah's house.

All the windows were dark, and no signs of the party remained. He took a deep breath, hoped his lifelong best friend still felt a shred of kindness for him, and threw a pebble at his second-floor window. The curtain moved and Noah's face appeared in the window. He looked sleepy. Ben waved up at him. Noah shook his head and disappeared, the curtain falling back into position. Desperation mounting in his chest, Ben threw another rock at the window. Noah's face reappeared, looking even less happy, if that was possible.

What? Noah mouthed at him. Ben put his hands

together in a *please* gesture. Noah rolled his eyes and held up his index finger to say *one minute*.

Ben waited. A few minutes later, Noah came around the back of his house wearing a sweatshirt over his pajamas. He walked across the lawn to Ben.

"Are you here to apologize again? That's why they invented texting, you know," Noah said, crossing his arms.

Ben swallowed hard. "You know I'm sorry. And I'll keep apologizing for, like, a month if you want me to. But that's not why I'm here."

Noah stared at him. When Ben didn't speak right away, Noah raised his eyebrows and held up his hands impatiently. "Then why are you here?"

"Hero and Scout. They're gone."

Noah's expression changed completely, from stubborn indifference to total shock.

"What do you mean, they're gone? Gone where?" Noah's jaw dropped in shock.

"I don't know. I left Scout in his crate in the backyard, and Hero was tied up to the tree. I've looked for them everywhere—all over town."

Noah shook his head, trying to understand. "Your parents didn't take them somewhere?"

"No." Ben looked down at the ground. "I had to tell my dad the dogs were here so he wouldn't be upset with me for losing them."

"Ben, you didn't lose them. Someone had to have taken them, right?"

Ben shrugged helplessly. None of this made any sense.

"Noah, I really need your help finding them."

Noah's face hardened again. "Sure. Now you're super sorry because you need my help."

"I was sorry before!" Ben said a little too loudly. Noah shushed him and looked nervously over his shoulder toward his house. It remained dark and quiet. "I'm not just sorry because I need your help," Ben went on, quieter this time. "I know I messed up really bad—but right now, I just really need to find the dogs, and I—" Ben could hear himself pleading. "I can't do it alone."

Noah stood silently for a moment, studying his friend.

"Ben, what's going on? You're acting kind of weird lately."

Ben exhaled slowly.

"I'm screwing up everywhere," he finally confessed.

"What does that mean?"

"That means I'm messing up at school, with my parents, at work, with the dogs. With you. It's like I just can't handle everything. My grades are seriously in trouble."

"For real?"

"Yeah. For real. Like, the school called my parents for real. My dad grounded me tonight. And whether Hero likes it or not, my parents won't let me keep Scout if I don't get it together." Ben kicked the grass in frustration. "Scout is all alone and so young. And someone hurt him on purpose—who could do that? Can you imagine how scared Scout must have been? And Hero would be so upset if something happened to Scout. Hero is my family. He's—I mean—he's Hero. He saved my life once. I can't just leave them out there somewhere, can I?"

Noah groaned. "You sure know how to make me feel bad. Let me get my bike." He disappeared up the driveway and came back a moment later. They hopped on their bikes and rode off. "What's the plan?"

"Um, I thought we'd try the animal shelter? Just to make sure they didn't end up there somehow."

"Good idea."

"It's the part after that I'm not so sure about."

"We'll figure it out," Noah said simply. "But I'm still really mad at you."

Ben was filled with gratitude for Noah. They biked down the empty streets toward the shelter, riding side by side through the darkness.

15

BEN POUNDED ON THE DOOR OF the animal shelter. It swung open, and bright fluorescent light spilled out onto the street. A man in medical scrubs stood in the doorway, his hair sticking up in multiple directions. He rubbed a hand over his eyes. He looked like they'd just woken him up. Ben blinked and explained why they were there.

"Come on in," the man said, waving a hand in the air.

Ben and Noah followed him down a long hallway, toward the sound of an animal symphony. They stepped into a vast room lined with rows of cages. The shelter worker handed Ben a beat-up notebook and asked him to sign in. Then he pointed to the right side of the room.

"Dogs are on that side," he said. "Hope you find the one you're looking for. I'll be at my desk if you need me." He headed off to the left.

Ben and Noah headed down the first aisle. A beagle mix stared at them longingly with big, droopy eyes. A white terrier with one brown spot on her back jumped up on her hind legs and pawed at the cage. Her entire bottom half wagged along with her tail. A rangy mutt with a gray muzzle tilted her head as they passed and let out a howl. Ben couldn't believe there were so many dogs. Every one of them looked sweeter than the last. Had all of them had a home once? Did someone stop loving them, or did they have to give them up? It was awful.

Ben and Noah saw dogs of every shape and size. There was the tiniest scrap of a dog—smaller than a Chihuahua, even, with a crazy underbite and fur spiking up from the top of its head. There was a creature that looked like a pair of eyes inside a huge ball of fur. And then there was the one that made Noah stop in his tracks and put his hand over his mouth. For a split second, Ben got excited—had he found Hero or Scout?

"Look at this dog," Noah said through his fingers.

Ben looked. It was a boxy gray-and-white puppy

with giant, floppy ears twice as big as his head. He looked like a baby, with a super-soft coat and a pink muzzle. He had the biggest eyes Ben had ever seen . . . and they were looking straight at Noah. The little dog wagged his tiny tail and skittered around his cage. He turned in circles and hopped up and down a couple of times.

"Who could abandon him?" Noah asked sadly. "Why doesn't anyone want all these dogs?"

Ben knew how his friend felt. He wished he could rescue every single one of them, but right then, he was focused on finding his own two dogs. Were they in danger? Were they locked up and scared, like these animals? He left Noah at the end of the row and turned the corner to the next aisle. He ran up and down the room, looking in every cage. His heart broke a little more at the sight of each dog, but he forced himself to move quickly. Finally, he got to the last cage.

Hero and Scout weren't there.

Desperate, Ben ran over to the shelter worker. The man looked up at him with a sympathetic expression. He probably saw people as panicked as Ben every day.

"Not here, kid?"

Ben shook his head and fought back tears.

"Sorry. If you want to leave me a description of your dog and your phone number, I can call you if he shows up."

"Two dogs," Ben said. "And I have a picture of them. Maybe you can tell me if you've seen them?" He pulled out his phone and swiped to a shot he'd taken of Scout sitting near Hero. Both dogs looked right into the camera.

The man studied the photo for a second. "I've seen the little guy, actually," he said.

"Really? When?"

"A few weeks ago."

That was before Ben and Hero found Scout in the woods.

"The dog wasn't here," the shelter worker went on, "but a guy came in looking for him. He left a picture." He dug through the piles of paper on his desk and pulled out a photo. He handed it to Ben.

The dog in the picture was Scout. He was looking sadly through the bars of a dog crate.

Ben was confused. His dad said no one had been looking for the puppy.

"Did he say it was his dog?" Ben asked.

"Actually, I was off that day. But one of the other

guys that works here told me about it 'cause it was kind of weird."

"Weird how?"

"Well, most people, if they're looking for their dog, they're real upset and want you to call them right away if any animal even looking like theirs comes in. But not this guy. I guess he didn't want to leave his number."

"Do you know what he looked like?"

"Sorry." The worker shook his head. "Like I said, I wasn't here." The guy's eyes lit up. "But his name would be on the sign-in sheet." He flipped back a few pages in the notebook and pointed to the right-hand column. "It was right around then."

Ben scanned the page. None of the names jumped out at him—until he got to the bottom of the column. There, in loopy, uneven handwriting, was a name he knew all too well: Jack Murphy.

"Thank you," Ben said, managing a weak smile. Anger flared up in his chest. His head was spinning. Why would Jack come looking for Scout? None of this made any sense.

Something wasn't right—he could feel it. And he knew what he had to do next.

16

BEN AND NOAH RODE HOME IN silence. The only sound was their bike wheels on the asphalt.

"It's a bummer that we didn't find them there," Noah said. "But we'll look more tomorrow."

Ben's mind was running in a thousand different directions at once, but he kept coming back to one thought. Something that had been nagging at him, even though he couldn't put his finger on why, exactly: Jack. Was he part of the dogfighting ring? It was the only explanation for all of this.

"This is going to sound crazy," he said.

"Um, crazier than the fact that we were just at the animal shelter at two A.M.?"

"I guess not." Ben paused. "I think Jack took my dogs."

"Whoa. You were right. That sounds crazy. Why would he do that?"

"His name was on that sign-in sheet at the shelter," Ben said.

"What?" Noah blurted out. "But that doesn't make sense—do you think he was looking for Scout before Scout was even . . . Scout? I mean, before you even found him?"

"I told you it sounded insane. But what if Jack is part of the dogfighting ring?"

"Ben, that's a serious accusation. And he's just a kid, like us."

"It's a crazy theory, I know," Ben said. "But he heard you remind me about your mom's party the other day, so he knew I wouldn't be home. Then I saw him outside my house last night, right before Hero and Scout disappeared, when I was heading to your house."

"Okay . . ."

"And he's sort of weird about Hero. It's like Jack wants him or something."

"Except for the part where Hero almost ate him at tryouts."

137

Even then, Ben thought, it was like Jack had wanted to upset Hero. He had to have known that if he threw the ball at Ben, Hero would get upset. Was he trying to get Hero riled up?

"Remember when Jack asked me if I would bet Hero?"

"Yeah, that was bizarre," Noah conceded. "So let's go talk to him. Tomorrow. Or later today, whatever it is."

The next day was Saturday, but Ben was up early. He could barely sleep. He was ready to go to Jack's before the sun came up, but he didn't want to go alone—and he didn't want to wake up Noah since he'd kept him out most of the night. He waited impatiently for his phone to ring. When Noah finally called around eleven and yawned into the phone that he was ready to go, Ben was on his bike within minutes.

Ben and Noah sat, bleary-eyed, on the curb across the street from Jack's house. They had rung the bell, but no one was home. They weren't bothering to hide. Ben planned to confront Jack right there on the sidewalk, in front of his mom or anyone who happened to pass by. It had been hours since his dogs had gone missing, and he was starting to feel desperate—and scared.

An hour passed. Ben was worried about getting

home on time. He was still grounded, but he'd told his parents he and Noah were going to do homework together. Ben was about to tell Noah to forget it when Jack rounded the corner on his bike. He was carrying something under one arm.

Ben waited until Jack pulled to a stop in front of his house. Jack hopped off his bike, and Ben could see what he'd been holding: a bag of dog food.

Ben was flooded with adrenaline. There was his proof. Jack was behind this.

"You'd better go home," he whispered to Noah through gritted teeth.

"What are you talking about?" he whispered back. "We've been waiting forever. I'm not lea—"

Ben didn't hear the rest of his sentence. He was already crossing the street. He could feel his blood rising. Rage was building in his chest, and his ears pounded.

"Hey!" Ben yelled out.

Jack spun around. His eyes narrowed when he saw Ben.

"What do you want?" Jack asked. He started to walk toward his house.

"I want my dogs!" Ben couldn't hide his anger.

Jack looked at Ben like he was nuts.

"Your dogs? What are you talking about? Why would I have your dogs?"

Ben froze. His head was spinning. Jack actually looked like he was telling the truth.

"Then what were you doing at my house last night? Why did you go to the animal shelter a couple of weeks ago?"

"I didn't know it was your house, honestly." Jack wasn't acting like his usual smug self. "I don't know my way around town yet, and I was just trying to get home." Jack shrugged. "Then all of a sudden you came flying down your driveway. I thought you'd think it was weird that I was there, so I got out of there fast."

Ben didn't know what to believe. Jack sounded so sincere. But the dog food . . .

"What's that for, then?" Ben pointed at the bag under Jack's arm.

"It's food," Jack spat, as if Ben had asked the stupidest question on earth. "For my dog."

"You—wait—" Ben stammered. "You have a dog?"

Jack turned and headed for his front door. He swung it open. Out limped an old, tired golden retriever. The fur around her muzzle was totally gray, and she moved slowly, like she was in pain. She whimpered a little and stuck her nose in Jack's palm. Her tail wagged slowly.

"This is my dog, Holly. She's really sick. I just went to get her prescription and some more food. And I went to the shelter a while back to donate some of her toys and stuff. She can't really play with anything anymore."

Ben's cheeks burned. He felt terrible, but he didn't know if he was more embarrassed, guilty, or panicked. If Jack didn't have his dogs, then who did?

Ben looked down at the ground.

"I'm sorry," Ben said. "Jack, I didn't know." He looked up at Jack, who stared off into the distance, one hand resting on Holly's head. "Man, you've been having a rough time lately, huh? Your parents, your dog . . ."

Jack didn't look at him. "I'm fine."

"Ben," Noah said from the sidewalk. "Let's go."

"I'm sorry," Ben repeated. He felt weird just leaving Jack there. "After I find Hero and Scout, I'll come back. Okay? But I gotta go. I'll . . . uh . . . I'll see you later."

Ben hopped on his bike and rode off, leaving Jack and his sweet old dog standing together on their front lawn.

17

BEN TOSSED AND TURNED ALL NIGHT. His sheets felt scratchy and hot. His pillow was lumpy. Every time he fell asleep, he woke up with a start, afraid that he had forgotten something. But he hadn't forgotten something—he had lost something. Two things. There was just a cold spot on the floor by his bed, where Hero used to sleep. And downstairs, an empty crate was a reminder that Scout was missing.

Sunday morning, Ben got out of bed at dawn, more exhausted than he'd ever been. His mom was already at the kitchen table, reading the paper and sipping her coffee. Even Erin was still asleep.

She was surprised to see Ben downstairs so early.

"Good morning, sunshine," she said, a quizzical look on her face. "Or should I say 'Good morning, thundercloud'?"

"Hey, Mom," he mumbled. He dropped into a chair across from her.

She scrunched up her face and studied him. "Ben, honey, are you okay? You don't look so hot."

Ben fought tears. He wished he could tell his mom everything. He felt alone and scared, but if he asked his parents for help finding the dogs, they would take Scout away—if he ever found him again, that was. And then Hero would be heartbroken, and it would all be Ben's fault. It was like a puzzle with no real solution. Ben didn't know what to do.

"I'm okay," he said, wishing he sounded more convincing. "It's just—well, you know, Mom . . ."

"Yes?"

"I just have a lot to do, and I don't know if I can get it all done. That's all." Ben exhaled. It wasn't a lie . . . it just wasn't exactly the whole truth.

His mom looked at him. Ben shifted in his chair and looked at the floor. He worried he'd said too much already.

"That doesn't sound like anyone in my family," his mom said firmly.

Ben's head shot up. He hadn't expected to hear those words.

"When your dad feels overwhelmed," she went on, "do you know what he does?"

Ben shook his head.

"Even if he's in the middle of an investigation, he stops, figures out what he's not doing right and how he could do it better, and he comes up with a new plan. He doesn't sit around feeling mopey, that's for sure," his mom said.

Ben absorbed her words. He *had* been spending an awful lot of time feeling sorry for himself—sorry that he wasn't getting his homework done, sorry that his parents had grounded him, sorry that they were threatening to take away Scout. His mom was right.

Suddenly Ben's thoughts were interrupted by the best sound he'd heard in his entire life: barking and scratching at the back door.

He let out a loud whoop and hopped out of his chair. He crossed the kitchen in two big steps and flung open the door.

Hero was back!

Hero stood in the doorway panting, one eye swollen. He held his left front paw up in the air ever so slightly, as if it hurt too much for him to put down. His beautiful coat was matted and dirty. Relief washed over Ben as he dropped to his knees and threw his arms around Hero's neck. The feel of Hero's warm fur and the sound of his breath brought Ben back to that night so many years ago, when the dog had appeared out of the darkness and Ben knew he was going to be okay. He never wanted to let go of Hero, who stood patiently while Ben hugged him.

"Are you okay, buddy?" Ben asked, pulling away and looking the dog up and down. "Poor guy," he muttered as he inspected Hero's injuries. They didn't seem too bad, thankfully. Hero licked Ben's face as Ben looked past him into the backyard. It was empty and quiet.

Scout wasn't there.

"You two sure missed each other," Ben's mom said, walking over and crouching down next to them. Ben nodded, struggling to hide his concern for Scout.

"Aw, Hero," she said, scratching Hero under the chin. "What happened to you, buddy?"

Ben's mind worked overtime to try to come up with a plausible explanation.

"Um, Noah said he got stuck in the hedge behind his house and got a little scratched up, that's all."

His mom eyed him skeptically. "Uh-huh" was all she said. Ben could tell she didn't entirely believe him, but luckily she didn't push it.

"Where's Scout?"

"Oh, he's still at Noah's," Ben said. "He's too little to walk home by himself, of course."

"Of course," his mom said slowly.

Ben needed to escape before she started asking more questions. "Actually, I think I'll go over there and see Scout, okay, Mom?"

"Let's clean Hero up a little first," she said.

She dabbed gently at Hero's eye with a wet washcloth and soaked his paw in a bowl of warm, salty water. Hero seemed to improve quickly.

Even though he was worried sick about Scout, Ben forced himself to remain outwardly calm. Besides, he knew, he had the best hope of finding Scout right here by his side: Hero.

If anyone could track Scout, Hero could.

Finally his mom kissed the top of Hero's head. "All set."

Ben raced for the door, Hero fast on his heels. "See you later, Mom."

"Ben," she called out after him. "Remember—you're

still grounded. You don't have a lot of time. You need to be back here in two hours, okay?"

"Okay!" Ben called.

Now that Hero was back, maybe they had a shot at finding Scout. Ben just hoped two hours would be enough time.

18

EVEN WITH A WOUNDED PAW, HERO ran faster than Ben could ever go on his bike.

All the way to Noah's, one question ran through Ben's mind over and over: If Hero was this banged up, what kind of shape would the puppy be in? It made him queasy to even think about it. Hero ran right up to Noah's front door and scratched at it. Noah dropped to his knees when he saw him.

"Hero! You're back!" He gave Hero a long hug, which the dog patiently endured. Noah pulled back, took Hero's head in his hands, and looked him right in the eye. "Where's Scout?" he asked firmly.

Hero leaped up and bolted across the lawn to the

curb. He stopped and looked back at Noah and Ben, his tail wagging frantically. He barked at them once, short and sharp, as if to say, *Let's go!*

Noah and Ben hopped on their bikes and followed Hero down the street. He led them out of the neighborhood, along the waterfront, and into a rural area outside of town. He turned off the main thoroughfare and onto a narrow, bumpy road. Ben's teeth rattled as his bike bounced up and down over the holes and rocks.

They came around a bend in the long road, and Ben saw a massive barn off in the distance. It was cavernous—the size of an airplane hangar—and dilapidated. As they got closer, Ben could see that giant chunks of its roof were missing. The exterior walls were covered in rust and dirt. The whole building seemed to sag to the left. Scattered around the perimeter were old industrial farming machines that clearly hadn't been used in a long time. Silos were crumbling, and long metal chutes had giant holes sagging open like gaping mouths. A couple of rusting tractors sat, frozen and long forgotten, nearby. Hero sat down in the road—what he was trained to do when he had tracked a subject to its final destination. He waited for Ben's command.

Ben studied the building and let out a long, low

whistle. The place was scary looking, but if Scout was in there, he was going in after him. He looked over at Noah.

"You don't have to go in with me," he said.

"Shut up. Let's go," Noah said.

Ben saw the same determination in his friend's face that he felt. The three of them moved silently toward the barn. They stopped behind one of the old, immobile tractors, out of view of the barn's double-wide front doors. The right-side door was ajar just a few inches. From his position, Ben could see people moving around inside. He heard muffled voices and distant barking.

"Okay. Hero, stay." Hero cocked his head at Ben. "Sorry, pal. I just don't want you to get hurt anymore. I can't lose you again." Ben's voice cracked. Hero sat down, but his ears pointed straight up. He sniffed at the air. Every muscle in his body was tensed and ready for action. He wanted to protect Ben, but this time it was Ben's turn to keep Hero safe.

Ben and Noah slipped inside the barn doors. Luckily an old pickup truck had been left to rust just inside the barn. They stood hidden behind it and let their eyes adjust to the dim lighting. Ben peered over the truck. The barn seemed even bigger inside than it had from the outside. From where they stood, Ben couldn't even see the other side of the building. It must have been a football field long, and the roof was at least twenty feet high.

Off to their right, a group of men stood in a half circle, around a ring of hay bales, their backs to Ben and Noah. The men were watching something near the ground. They cheered and raised their fists in the air. At first Ben couldn't see what they were looking at—it was just a blur of motion. But then he heard it: Snarling. Growling. Pained yelping and crying. He smelled the sharp tang of blood in the air.

It was a dogfight.

Ben was disgusted. What kind of psychos would watch dogs tear each other apart? Suddenly a horrible thought occurred to him, and he felt clammy with fear. Scout. These idiots couldn't possibly let a puppy fight— would they? What if Scout was in the ring right now? Blood pounded in his ears as he squinted and tried to see the dogs in the ring. They were moving so fast, but Ben could tell that they were both big. Neither one was Scout—but it could be Scout's turn at any moment.

They had to move fast. Noah must have had the same thought, because he nudged Ben with his elbow and pointed toward the opposite side of the barn. There were two rows of metal cages, stacked on top of each other. Inside them, dogs of all ages, sizes, and breeds turned in circles, pawed at the latches, or whimpered sadly. The worst ones just sat quietly, staring blankly, as if they'd accepted their horrible fate. There must have been close to fifty dogs there.

"Let's split up," Ben whispered to Noah. "You start from the back, and I'll start from the front."

Noah nodded. Silently, they moved along the edge of the building toward the cages. Ben stopped at the first row, and Noah continued on. Ben watched him go until he was out of sight.

Ben turned to the imprisoned dogs, and his heart nearly broke. Their faces were scarred and bloody. Their ears were ripped and even missing. Their bodies bore the marks of many injuries. Even worse than their wounds, though, were their eyes. They gazed at Ben with a combination of desperation and fear. Some wagged their tails when they saw him, but many just looked at him, like they couldn't possibly be happy to see a human being ever again. Ben swore to himself silently that after he saved Scout, he'd find a way to come back and save the rest of them.

Ben forced himself to keep moving. He scanned the cages from top to bottom, right to left, looking for

Scout. He was almost done with the second row of dogs when he found him. Scout was in the last cage in his row, on the bottom, cowering in the back corner. The sound of his soft whimpering was horrible. Ben dropped to his knees in front of the cage.

When he saw Ben, Scout didn't jump up right away—he just looked at Ben, crying and shaking. His fur was caked with dirt. Ben almost couldn't bear the sadness in Scout's eyes.

After a moment, Scout got to his feet and made his way toward the front of the cage. He whined and stuck the tip of his nose through the metal. Ben reached a few fingers in and rubbed Scout's chin. Scout licked his hand. This was the worst thing that could have happened to the puppy, Ben knew. He had worked so hard to be comfortable with Ben and his family, to trust people again. And here he was, mistreated and left to suffer. Again.

"It's okay, Scout," Ben whispered. "I'm gonna get you out of here."

Ben tried to slide open the latch on Scout's cage. It wouldn't give. He looked at it more closely and saw that someone had used a plastic cable tie to secure the door. There was no way the dogs were getting out of these cages. Ben fumbled around in his pockets for something to cut the tie. His keys would probably do the trick.

"Well, look who it is," said a deep voice behind him. Ben froze with fear. "Stand up."

Ben stood up. Something about the man's voice felt familiar, but Ben's heart was pounding so hard that he couldn't place it.

"Turn around."

Ben turned around. It was Mitch—the tall man with the cold blue eyes who Ben had seen twice now: once at the car lot, and once outside Mitch's house. All the bits and pieces of the last couple of weeks began to fall into place. Mitch ran this dogfighting ring, not Jack. And Scout had been Mitch's dog.

It was the only explanation that accounted for all the weird things that had happened. Mitch had seen Scout at the car lot and recognized him as one of his dogs. Mitch was the one who drove the black SUV by Ben's house—and then he must have followed Ben to the police station. Mitch was waiting for an opportunity to get Scout back—and he got it when Scout ran away from the station. He must have picked him up in his car, which explained how Scout got to Mitch's house so fast. And Mitch was the man who had gone to the shelter with a picture of Scout. He hadn't left his name because he was part of an illegal dogfighting ring.

It also explained why Scout got upset every time he saw Mitch.

Mitch was behind all of this.

"That's my dog," Ben said angrily. "And I want him back."

Mitch let out a dry laugh. "Actually, kid, that's my dog. I've been trying to get him back without anyone getting hurt, but you just won't give up, will you?"

Ben clenched and unclenched his fists. His nostrils flared as he inhaled and exhaled sharply, trying to control himself. *Stay present. Stay calm. Figure it out.*

"I didn't catch your name the other day," Mitch said, nastiness seeping into his voice. Ben didn't say anything. He kept his eyes locked on Mitch's. "You're the silent type, I see." Mitch put his face just inches from Ben's. Ben could feel Mitch's hot breath. He resisted the urge to take a step back.

"I told you the other day you should fight those dogs of yours," Mitch snarled. "But you thought they were too good for it. Well, guess what? Your big dog is a brawler. And that one"—he gestured toward Scout—"he's tiny, but he's a tough son of a gun. I thought he'd be a good bait dog, but turns out you've trained him up real nice for me. So I guess I owe you one. He's gonna have his first real fight today."

Ben felt ill.

A flicker of motion over Mitch's shoulder distracted Ben. It was Noah. He stood in the darkness toward the back of the barn, motioning to Ben. Ben pretended to be staring off into the distance and considering Mitch's words. Noah shook his head and put a finger to his lips. *He doesn't know I'm here,* Noah was telling Ben. *And let's keep it that way.* Noah pointed at Scout's cage, then at himself. *I'll get Scout.* Ben quickly formulated a plan.

"You seem like a nice kid," Mitch said, "so I'm going to give you one last chance to get out of here without getting hurt. And I assume you're not stupid enough to tell anyone what you saw here today. Normally I'm not a very trusting person, but I'm making an exception this one time. So you don't get any more chances—you hear me?"

"Yeah, I hear you," Ben replied. "I'll go." Ben took one step backward, and Scout went crazy in his cage. The puppy whined and howled desperately. The sound was like a punch to Ben's gut.

"It's okay, buddy," he said to Scout. "You're gonna be okay."

19

"STUPID KID," MITCH GROWLED AT BEN as he shoved him through the barn door. "You'd better get home. I bet your mama's looking for you." He slammed the door behind Ben.

Ben ran to his bike, which was still leaning against the old tractor. Hero hopped to his feet.

"Sorry, Hero. You need to stay. Stay." Hero sat back down and watched Ben with big, expectant eyes.

Ben rode his bike quickly around the perimeter of the barn. There had to be another door somewhere.

Two-thirds of the way around the building, and he had found several pairs of barn doors—all of them bolted shut with heavy, rusted chains and padlocks. Ben was just about to give up when he rounded the final corner. There, at the back of the building, was a small, single door, painted the same color as the sides of the building. This one didn't have a lock—they must have overlooked it. Even Ben had almost whizzed right by it.

Ben leaned his bike against the side of the barn and mapped out a plan. He'd go back into the barn this way, out of sight of the men at the front of the building. He would find Noah and Scout, and he would get them out through this door.

It was the only plan he had.

The door was rusted shut. Ben twisted the handle and pulled hard until it jerked open with a loud screech. He froze, but no one came for him. Mitch and the others probably hadn't heard him over the horrible snarling and growling of the dogs in the ring—and the raucous cheering of the crowd.

Ben stepped into the dimly lit barn. The sound of his own fast breathing was loud in his ears. He closed his eyes and prepared himself for whatever was about to happen. The only thing he knew for sure was that he and Noah needed to get Scout out of there before it was the puppy's turn in that ring. At the front of the barn, the sound of dogs tearing at each other reached a ferocious pitch. Suddenly, the fight was over, and Ben heard one of the dogs wailing and whimpering. It sounded like the animal was hurt—badly. Ben's stomach turned.

Half of the men gathered around the ring cheered. The other half booed loudly. While they were distracted, Ben darted silently toward the rows of cages. Had Noah gotten Scout yet?

He hadn't. Scout was still in his cage. The puppy cowered at the back, his whole body shaking. When he saw Ben, he hopped up and ran to the front of the cage, whimpering desperately.

"Shhhhh . . . Scout, quiet," Ben whispered. He looked around—Noah was nowhere to be seen. The ruckus by the fighting pit was dying down, and there was a lull in the noise—and the distraction. Ben had to get Scout out of his cage fast. He pulled his key ring out of his jeans pocket and started hacking at the plastic cable tie with his house key. Scout nosed at his fingers through the metal bars of the cage.

Snap. The cable tie gave way. Ben opened the cage door, and Scout leaped into his arms, wiggling excitedly.

"You're okay, buddy," Ben said softly to the pup. He cradled Scout in his arms. "Let's get you out of here." Ben turned to head toward the back of the barn.

Mitch stood right behind him. And this time, he had a knife.

Ben's breath caught in his throat. He suddenly understood what it was like to feel real fear. The kind of fear that sent your brain into overdrive and made your arms and legs freeze in place.

Ben heard his dad's voice in his head. *Breathe, Ben. Think.*

Ben wasn't sure how that advice was supposed to work when there was a man pointing a blade right at him, but he realized that his chest hurt. He'd forgotten to breathe. He inhaled sharply and exhaled slowly. It worked. He felt more in control of his body. His mind felt clearer. He gripped Scout tightly and tried to plan an escape route . . . but his feet were still paralyzed. He was too scared to move.

"I've really had it with you." Mitch snarled. "You just don't know when to quit, do you?"

Scout growled at Mitch from Ben's arms. Ben gripped the puppy tightly.

"Why can't you just forget about this dumb dog?" Mitch said.

Ben found his voice. "He's not dumb," Ben said angrily. "And I am not going to let you send him into that ring to get killed."

Mitch's lips turned up in a cold smile. "I'll make a deal with you," Mitch said. "Let's put him in the ring so you can see what a scrappy little fighter this pup is. If he wins, I get to keep him. If he loses, you get to take him." Mitch let out a harsh laugh. "Well, whatever's left of him, that is."

"You're disgusting." Ben's voice was calm, but his mind was racing. There was still a knife in front of him, but he didn't care. There was no way he was letting Scout fight. He had to think of a way out of this.

Before Ben knew what was happening, Mitch's hand flew out and snatched Scout from his arms.

"No!" Ben shouted.

With an angry yelp, Scout bit Mitch hard on the arm. Mitch screamed.

Suddenly, Ben saw a flash in the shadows behind Mitch. It was a blur, and it was getting closer. Mitch wasn't paying attention—he was looking at the bite wound on his arm, which was oozing blood, his face screwed up in anger. The blur kept coming, and then it was leaping into the air toward Mitch's back.

Ben sucked in his breath when he saw who it was: It was Hero!

Hero soared at top speed, front paws extended, teeth

bared, and ears pointed back. He was in full attack mode, and he had one target: Mitch.

Mitch had no idea what was coming. He let out a confused grunt as Hero landed on him. Ben watched Mitch's eyes grow big as his body fell forward, Hero on his back with his teeth clamping down on the back of Mitch's neck.

Scout flew from Mitch's grasp and skittered away. Mitch fell facedown onto the concrete floor, his head hitting the ground with a sickening thump. Hero stood on top of him, growling angrily. Mitch was out cold.

"Attaboy, Hero!" Ben said. He scanned the room for Scout. He spotted the puppy running toward the back of the barn. "Hero, find Noah!" he said before bolting after Scout. Hero darted off in search of him. As Ben closed in on the puppy, he heard the sound of paws on the concrete behind him. Had Hero found Noah so fast?

He looked back over his shoulder and nearly tripped when he saw who—or what—was chasing him. Fast on his heels were two of the most ferocious-looking beasts he had ever seen. They raced toward him at top speed, their ears flat against their heads and their sharp teeth flashing. They were bloodthirsty demons.

And it was his blood they wanted.

In the distance, Ben heard a man shouting, "Mitch! Mitch—are you okay, man? Wake up!" One of the other men had found Mitch lying on the ground, which meant that in a few seconds, the dogs wouldn't be the only ones coming after Ben.

Ben couldn't see Scout anywhere. The dogs were getting closer. Soon they were going to have him cornered in the back of the barn. Ben ran through his options: He could save himself and run through the back door, but then he'd be leaving Noah, Hero, and Scout inside. He could never do that to them. He could try to fight off the dogs, but with what? He had no weapons, nothing.

Ben was rapidly approaching the back wall of the barn and a miserable fate. He could practically smell the dogs' sour breath, and their angry growls vibrated in his bones. They would be closing in on him in three . . . two . . . He waited for the pain of their teeth sinking into his flesh.

Nothing happened.

Ben heard a loud and horrifying yelp behind him. He skidded to a halt and spun around. One of the dogs was on the ground, bleeding. The other was crouched down low, circling his opponent: Hero.

Hero faced the dog, baring his teeth, a savage growl

emanating from his throat. All the fur along his back bristled.

Hero had saved Ben once again. And now he was putting himself in harm's way to buy Ben time to go find the others.

Ben hesitated. He hated to leave his dog locked in a showdown with that rabid-looking monster, but he also understood exactly what Hero was doing. No—as much as Ben wanted to stay and help Hero, that wasn't what his dog wanted. Hero wanted him to go save Scout and Noah.

Ben took off running back toward the front of the barn. He stayed close to the wall, in the shadows. Behind him, he heard Hero ruthlessly attacking the dog, followed by agonized cries. He pushed the gruesome sounds out of his mind and moved forward.

He looked around for Noah or Scout, but he didn't see either of them. Up ahead, he saw a man helping Mitch to his feet. Ben stopped and pressed himself against the wall. But he wasn't fast enough.

"There he is!" Mitch called out. "Hey, kid—stop right there!"

Ben was out of time.

He stepped forward and raised his hands in the air.

Mitch stumbled toward him, one hand holding his head, the other pointing the knife at Ben. Mitch's face was filled with rage and pain. The other man followed him as he closed in on Ben.

Ben just wanted to rewind everything, or at least hit *pause*. Just for a second, so he could clear his head and figure out what to do. But life didn't work that way. Ben exhaled. He tried to slow down his racing heart. He tried to push aside all the useless fears and worries. He tried to think.

Ben glared at Mitch, wishing he could communicate with his eyes all the disgust and hatred he felt. Mitch was close enough now that Ben could see a look in Mitch's eyes that made Ben's blood run cold. Mitch wanted to hurt Ben. Badly.

Ben swallowed hard. He tried not to let his fear show. He didn't want to give this idiot the pleasure of seeing him scared. He took sharp breaths through his nose. He would face whatever was about to happen with his head held high. But he felt terrible for his parents and Erin—for whatever he was about to put them through. He just hoped they would understand that he had been trying to save Hero and Scout.

Ben's mouth was dry, and his pulse was pounding in his neck. He kept his eyes locked on Mitch's.

"You're all out of chances," Mitch said, his voice weaker than before.

"Hey, meatheads! Over here!" came a shout off to Ben's left. The men spun toward the sound. Noah stood about ten feet away. In one hand, he held Scout. With the other, he gripped Hero's collar, holding the dog back as he strained forward, bleeding from wounds on his nose and shoulder. Hero growled at Mitch.

"You want this puppy back?" Noah yelled at Mitch. "Come and get him."

Mitch lurched toward Noah and the dogs, followed closely by his henchman.

Noah stared them down as they closed in on him. The men were just a couple of feet away. "Oh," he said with a wicked grin, "and you can have this one too."

And with that, Noah let go of Hero's leash.

20

"GO GET 'EM, HERO," NOAH CRIED.

Hero dropped into a fighting stance, his front feet splayed out and his chest low to the ground. His eyes burned with hatred, and when he opened his mouth to snarl at the men, Ben saw blood on his teeth from the other dogs.

Mitch held his hands out in front of him. "It's okay, buddy," he said in a voice that was so obviously fake it made Ben want to barf. "We're all friends here," Mitch cooed. Hero growled and tensed every muscle in his body. The fur on his back stood on end. Hero launched himself into the air, straight at Mitch. Ben sucked in his breath as he watched Hero soar, pure muscle and power and instinct.

Ben watched the next few moments as if they happened in slow motion. Hero planted his front paws in Mitch's chest. Mitch grunted as the wind got knocked out of him. He tipped over backward and fell into the man right behind him. The two men toppled like dominoes.

Hero landed on top of Mitch, his paws still on the man's chest. Mitch wailed in pain as his head smacked the concrete again. The knife popped out of his hand and went spinning across the floor into the darkness, far out of his reach. Hero bared his teeth in Mitch's face and let out a low warning growl. Mitch covered his face with his arm, protecting himself from Hero. The other man pushed himself backward, terrified of the big dog.

Ben knew what Hero was doing. This was their window to escape, once and for all.

"Noah!" he yelled, gesturing to him to follow. Clutching Scout firmly under his arm, Noah ran toward Ben. "There's a door back there," Ben said, jerking his thumb toward the back of the barn.

"Let's go," Noah said, "before that moron gets up."

With a last look at Hero, who still stood guard over Mitch, Ben took off running. Noah followed close on his heels. They ran past the two dogs Hero had fended off, who lay on their sides, panting heavily, too injured to try to stop Ben and Noah.

They were almost at the back door when Ben heard the sound of paws on concrete behind them. He turned to look—Hero was catching up to them! That meant they could all get out at once, which was good. But it also meant Hero wasn't keeping the men from following them anymore, which was bad.

"Did they get away?" Mitch's angry voice rang out across the barn. Ben heard heavy footsteps.

"What do we do?" Noah's voice was tinged with panic.

"We can't leave Hero," Ben said firmly.

But the men were close. Ben grabbed Noah's sleeve and pulled him into the shadows by the door. Hero had stopped to face Mitch and the others.

"Hero!" Ben whispered. Hero's ear flicked at the sound of Ben's voice, but he stood still. Hero was going to hold off the men. Ben was terrified for his dog, but he knew he didn't want to waste Hero's sacrifice either. He tapped Noah and pointed to the door. Noah followed his gaze and nodded in understanding. Ben held up his index finger, indicating that they should wait. Noah nodded again.

Hero growled. Mitch and the other man skidded to a stop right in front of him.

Ben held his breath.

Mitch looked jumpy, like he was prepared for Hero to pounce on him again. The other guy stood even farther back. Mitch took a tentative step forward and reached out a hand to grab Hero's collar. Hero went quiet and ducked his head.

For a second, Ben thought that Hero was letting Mitch catch him. What was he doing—Hero would never give up, would he? But then it clicked: Hero was tricking Mitch. He was going to let him get close, and then . . .

Hero snarled and snapped his head sideways, latching on to Mitch's calf with his powerful jaw. Mitch cried out in pain, but he couldn't get away. Hero held on tight, his eyes narrow slits.

"Okay, Hero!" Ben yelled out. Hero released Mitch's leg, tearing off a large scrap of his pants as he did. Mitch doubled over in agony and fell to the ground.

"Get him!" Mitch yelled to the other man, who looked petrified. Hero's lip curled up, revealing his sharp fangs, and the man backed away. Hero was about to lunge at him when Scout suddenly let out a fierce bark from his spot in Noah's arms. Ben had never heard Scout bark like that before—he sounded like a much bigger and older dog. Scout wanted to help Hero.

Hero's ears twitched. Distracted by Scout's cry, Hero half turned his head in Scout's direction. It was just for a second, but that was all it took. The man saw his opportunity and bolted toward Hero. He reached for Hero's collar but missed and went falling forward. He landed on top of the dog, tackling him to the ground and pinning Hero under all his weight. Hero let out a horrible squeal of pain—a sound that turned Ben's stomach. Hero was hurt.

"No!" Ben cried out. Desperation shot through him. He looked around frantically for something—anything—that would help him save Hero. Ben spotted something leaning against the back wall by the door. He reached for it—it was a long, rusty shovel with a splintered wooden handle. He hefted it with both hands and ran toward Hero and the man who still lay on top of him. Before the man had time to react, Ben swung the shovel high in the air and brought it down fast onto his head. With a groan, the man passed out cold and fell to the side, off Hero.

Ben dropped to his knees next to his dog. Hero lay

still, panting shallowly, his tongue hanging out of his mouth. He looked dazed.

"It's okay, Hero." Ben choked up. "I'm here."

Noah raced over and, with the hand that wasn't holding Scout, helped Ben scoop up Hero. He winced a little when they moved him. Hero looked up at Ben. Ben held his dog's gaze and fought tears.

"Let's get you out of here," Ben said.

Holding Hero tightly in his arms, Ben led Noah and Scout to the back door, and they scrambled through it, to safety.

21

BEN AND NOAH SAT SLUMPED IN the molded plastic chairs of the veterinarian's waiting room. A television droned on, high up in the corner. The women behind the reception desk chatted about their lives. Phones rang, and cell phones chirped with incoming messages. Ben's phone buzzed in his pocket. It was probably his parents wondering where he was.

Other people in the waiting room stared at Ben and Noah, who were covered in dirt and dust from the barn. Ben didn't care. It was all a blur to him. All he cared about was Hero. Hero had seemed so out of it when they burst through the vet's doors.

Would he survive? Had Ben killed his own dog? The

medical techs had taken Hero from him immediately and pushed Ben away. They had run with Hero through a door, and he hadn't heard from them since. It felt like they'd been waiting a lifetime.

Whatever happened to Hero, it was Ben's fault. The guilt and worry were a physical pain in Ben's chest, and his limbs felt like they weighed a thousand pounds each. He had never felt so drained in his entire life. Scout slept on Noah's lap, his body twitching with his dreams. Noah stared off into the distance.

Ben had asked the receptionists about Hero a couple of times, and they just kept saying they'd let him know as soon as they heard from the doctor.

Ben rubbed his face with his hands and let out a long exhale. He slipped his phone from his pocket and texted his mom and dad. He wasn't ready to tell them everything yet—he would, eventually.

Ben knew he deserved whatever consequences were coming his way for going after Hero and Scout alone, for putting Noah at risk, and for being out past his curfew. He didn't care. There was no amount of punishment in the world that was bad enough for what he'd done that day, or that would make him feel worse than he already did. Right now, he just needed his parents' help.

Hero hurt really bad, he wrote, his hands shaking. *Don't know if he's okay. Please come to vet.* Tears filled his eyes. He almost couldn't see the words as he hit *send*.

Ben sat back in his chair. His phone lit up instantly with a reply from his mom. They were on their way. He felt some small measure of relief that they would be there soon. The door next to the reception desk swung open, and a man in scrubs stepped through it. He held a medical chart in his hand. "Landry?" he read from the chart.

Ben and Noah jumped up and ran over to him. Scout tumbled off Noah's lap and landed on the floor with a clatter of toenails. He waggled after them and sat down on top of Ben's left foot.

"That's me," Ben said. "Is he okay? Is Hero going to be okay?" Noah gripped his arm.

The doctor smiled at them, and Ben sucked in his breath.

"Hero is going to be fine. He has a mild concussion, and his leg is sprained. We've patched up his cuts and bruises. But I think he's going to heal nicely."

Noah pumped a fist in the air and let out a "Yes!" Ben grinned from ear to ear.

"That's amazing," he said.

175

"But listen," the vet added in a serious tone. "Hero is going to need a lot of rest over the next few days."

"Sure—no problem." Ben nodded. Scout yipped at him from the floor. Ben leaned down to pick up the puppy, stroking his head to quiet him.

"You can take him home soon." The doctor looked past Ben to the waiting room. "Are your parents here?"

"They're on their way."

The vet clapped a hand on Ben's shoulder.

"You did good, son. You did the right thing getting Hero here as fast as you did."

Ben wanted to tell the doctor that it was all his fault—he was the reason Hero got hurt in the first place. But he just nodded and muttered his thanks. Someone came up in the doorway behind the vet.

"Excuse me," said a familiar voice. The doctor stepped aside to let someone out of the back rooms of the office. Ben was shocked to see that it was Jack.

Jack's face was red, and his eyes were puffy. It looked like he'd been crying. He was staring at something in his hands, but looked up and saw Ben.

"Ben?" Jack said.

"Hi, Jack," Ben said, too exhausted to care about any bad blood between them. Ben looked at what Jack was holding. He was clutching a worn leather dog collar with a tag dangling from it. Something registered in Ben's tired brain. His eyes shot back up to meet Jack's.

"Your dog—Holly?" Ben asked quietly.

Jack nodded, tears filling his eyes.

"She was my best friend," Jack said. "But she was really old and sick, and we had to . . ." He trailed off. His mom appeared in the doorway behind him, holding a bunch of papers in her hand. She put her arm around Jack's shoulders to lead him toward the door.

Jack started to walk away, but turned back to Ben.

"I'm sorry," Jack said. "About before."

"It's okay," Ben replied. "Me too."

Jack looked at Scout in Ben's arms and gave a faint half smile. "What's his name again?"

"Scout," Ben said. "Want to pet him?"

Jack nodded and ran a hand over Scout's soft coat. Scout sniffed at Jack's hand. The puppy jumped up and, while Ben held him around the belly, put his front paws on Jack's chest. Wagging his tail, Scout reached his nose forward and licked the salty tears from Jack's cheeks.

"He's sweet," Jack said with a strangled laugh.

"Yeah, thanks," Ben said.

"Come on, honey," Jack's mom said to her son. "Let's get you home."

"See you later, Scout. Bye, Ben." Jack turned and walked out with his mom.

Ben's parents and sister came running through the door, their faces strained with worry. Ben fell into his mother's arms, and his dad hugged them both.

"He's okay," Ben said, his voice muffled.

"Oh, thank goodness!" his mom cried, sniffling a little.

"Yay, Hero!" Erin shouted.

Woof! Scout barked from Ben's arms inside the huddle. Everyone laughed, and Ben's parents broke free to talk to the doctor. While Erin and Noah played with Scout, Ben looked out the front windows and saw Jack getting into his mom's car in the parking lot. His shoulders were slumped, and his head hung low. He looked so sad and . . . something else.

Lonely.

It occurred to Ben that he'd never really seen Jack hanging out with any other kids—and Jack had said he had nothing else to do the other night but walk around town, alone. It was hard to move to a new place and start a new school in the middle of the semester. Maybe

Jack hadn't handled it perfectly—he'd been a little aggressive, that was for sure. But he was probably just scared. Something Ben could relate to now, better than ever before.

It was late by the time Ben's dad carried a groggy Hero to the truck and got him settled in the backseat. Noah's dad had long since picked him up. Erin and Ben's mom were falling asleep sitting up in the truck. Ben climbed into the back and, careful not to bump Hero's bandaged leg, wrapped both arms around his dog's neck, and buried his face in Hero's fur.

Hero had saved his life again. And Ben would never forget it.

22

THE NEXT MORNING, BEN DIDN'T THINK it would be physically possible for him to make it through an entire day of school. He had never been so tired in his entire life—and he hoped he'd never be that tired again.

He stumbled downstairs for breakfast. His mom and Erin were already at the table.

"Morning, Benny," Erin said between slurps of cereal.

"Morning, Sis."

"Morning, honey," his mom said.

"Hey, Mom." He grabbed a bowl and dumped a mountain of cereal into it.

"Your dad's been at the station since before dawn. He

just called. They raided the barn overnight and found all the dogs."

"Just the dogs?" Ben asked nervously.

"Just the dogs, honey. All thanks to the statement you gave last night. Why?"

"Oh, no reason." Ben tried to look happy. He didn't want his mom to think there was any more to the story than what he'd already told his parents. After they'd gotten Hero settled and Scout in his crate, Ben had just wanted to go to sleep. But, understandably, his parents had lots of questions. Ben hadn't lied, exactly. He'd told his parents the truth—just not all of the truth. He'd mentioned that there were a bunch of guys there, and he'd given them a description of Mitch. But he'd held back the fact that he and Mitch had interacted as much as they had. He didn't tell them that he'd met Mitch before . . . or that Mitch had held a knife on him.

He hadn't wanted to freak out his parents any further. But now Ben was realizing that he'd been counting on the fact that Mitch would get caught when the cops went to bust up the dogfighting ring. Except that hadn't happened, which meant Mitch was still out there—and he knew exactly who had sent the cops. Ben.

Ben swallowed hard.

"Ben?" His mom was staring at him. "You okay?"

"Huh?" He plastered a smile on his face. "Oh yeah, of course. Just tired. That's great news that they saved all those dogs."

She eyed him quizzically for a moment.

"Yeah," she said. "It is great news. They're out looking for the guys behind it, but that might take some time."

"I'd better get to school," Ben said, standing up suddenly.

"Benny, you didn't eat your breakfast!" Erin said.

"I'm not hungry. But thanks, Sis," Ben said. He snatched up his backpack and headed out.

As soon as he set foot in school, though, Mitch was far from his mind. Ben and Noah were instantly swarmed by what seemed like every student there. The kids shouted out their names and high-fived them. Ben and Noah jostled their way down the hall to their lockers, but every couple of feet, someone else stopped them.

"Dude! I heard you busted, like, seventeen seriously bad guys!"

"No, that wasn't wha—" Ben tried to say.

"Noah, did you really save all those dogs all by yourself?"

"No, I didn't d—" he started before someone else cut him off.

"My mom said you let a hundred dogs loose."

"There weren't a hund—"

"How did you even know where to find them?"

"Actually, Hero, my dog—"

"Are you like a detective or something, Noah?"

"Landry for president!"

"Man," Ben said to Noah as soon as they broke free from the crowd, "if only they knew what really happened."

"No kidding." Noah peered back down the hallway at the sea of students. "They'd be so disappointed."

"It wasn't half as cool as they're making it sound," Ben said.

"And Hero and Scout should get all the credit," Noah replied.

"And you," Ben said, punching Noah on the shoulder. "You were amazing."

"Thanks, Ben." Noah shrugged. "You were too."

"How are we going to convince everyone that we're actually not that impressive?" Ben asked.

"I don't think they really care about the facts." Noah laughed. "Their version is way more dramatic."

"Maybe I like their story better than the truth anyway." Ben sighed. "I mean, it ended well, but it was kind of awful while it was happening, wasn't it?"

"You can say that again," Noah said.

"Uh, Noah, they still haven't caught Mitch." Ben hated even saying the words out loud.

"Seriously?" Noah grimaced. "That's terrible."

"I'm sure they'll get him soon," Ben said, trying to sound convincing.

"I hope so," Noah said. "But for now, whether we're heroes or not, we'd better get to English."

Ben tried to focus in class, but he couldn't stop replaying the events of the night before in his mind: Scout locked up and scared. The fear of not knowing where Noah was for so long. Hero putting himself in danger again and again, just to save Ben, Noah, and Scout. The anger in Mitch's voice as he yelled for Ben, and the sound of Mitch's footsteps coming closer. The sight of the knife, hovering in the air right in front of his face. The certainty that Mitch was about to hurt him.

Mitch. Ben suddenly remembered that he was still out there. He had to physically shake his head to get the image of that cold, cruel man out of it.

During his free period, Ben found a quiet bench

outside and tried to distract himself with the novel he had to finish for English.

"Hey, Ben." Ben looked up to find Jack standing there.

"Hey, Jack." In the weirdness of the day, Ben had forgotten about Jack's dog. "How're you doing? I mean—never mind. That's a dumb question."

"It's okay. I'm okay. I mean, I will be. Thanks."

"I'm glad."

"I heard about the dogfighting ring," Jack said. "I didn't realize when I saw you last night, that you'd just been . . . you know. Dealing with that. Nice work."

"Thanks. Honestly, Noah, Hero, and Scout are the real heroes."

"Is that how Hero got hurt?" Jack asked. "Is he okay?"

Ben pictured Hero looking so scared and out of it as they rushed him to the vet.

"Yeah," he said. "He's going to be okay. He's home now."

"That's good," Jack said. "So I heard he's, like, some kind of Superdog or something."

Ben grinned. "Something like that. He's a police dog. He's trained for search and rescue and other, you know, police stuff."

"That's really cool." Jack looked impressed.

"I'm trying to train Scout too," Ben said. "Not to be a police dog, just to be a dog dog. But it's harder than I thought it would be."

"If you need any help, maybe I could learn how to train too," Jack said with a shrug. "My mom and I might get a new puppy. Well, not right away, but soon."

Ben knew how scared he'd felt when Hero and Scout were missing and he was afraid he might lose them. He couldn't imagine how sad Jack felt right now.

"That'd be great. I can use all the help I can get," Ben said. "You could come over after school this week and I'll show you the basics. Maybe you can help me build a better obstacle course."

Jack's face brightened.

"Sounds cool."

"Great," Ben said. With a wave, Jack headed off.

Ben stumbled through the rest of the day. As soon as sixth period was over, he headed straight home. He couldn't wait to collapse onto the living room floor and spend the rest of the afternoon hanging out with Hero and Scout.

23

"ANYBODY HOME?" BEN SWUNG THE DOOR shut behind him.

"In here," his dad called from the kitchen.

Ben found his parents seated at the kitchen table, worried expressions on their faces. Hero struggled to his feet and hobbled over to greet Ben. Scout ran frantic little circles around Hero, yapping at his heels as if to tell him to sit down and take it easy. Ben patted them both.

"Sit, Hero," Ben said. "You need to rest." Hero seemed more than happy to drop to the floor and put his head down on his paws. "Hey, Mom. Hey, Dad. What's up—is everything okay?"

His dad ran a hand through his hair and sighed. "They've rounded up a bunch of the guys who were at the barn last night."

"That's great!" Ben said. He exhaled a huge sigh of relief. "But you guys don't look happy . . . what's wrong?"

"Well," his dad went on, "they got this Mitch character's second-in-command."

Ben pictured the large goon who had fallen on top of Hero. He had a few choice words for him, that was for sure.

"But they can't find Mitch," his dad finished. "He's just disappeared. And we don't have anything to go on."

Ben's stomach churned. The thought of Mitch still out there made him feel nauseous.

"Sit down, honey," Ben's mom said.

Ben sat between his parents.

"Son," his dad said, looking him directly in the eye, "is there anything you haven't told us? Anything you might know that could help us find this guy?"

No one said a word for a moment. Ben's mom took his hand in hers. Tears in his eyes, Ben inhaled and held his breath for a few seconds. When he exhaled, he began talking. This time, he told his parents everything.

He told them that Scout was Mitch's dog. That Mitch

had seen him with Scout at the used car lot. Mitch must have followed them to the police station and snatched Scout after the siren scared the puppy and he ran off. Ben told them about how he and Hero followed Scout to Mitch's house—and that Mitch was the one who had taken Hero and Scout from the Landrys' house. And finally, he confessed that Mitch had pulled a knife on him at the barn.

Ben left nothing out. When he was done, he felt an overwhelming sense of relief—for not having to keep secrets anymore, and because he felt so much less alone. His mom gave his hand a squeeze.

"I know you're going to be mad at me for all this, guys," he said. "And that's okay—I deserve it. But right now, all I care about is catching this guy. He's . . . awful. And it's all my fault that he's gone. I should have told you this sooner."

His dad pulled Ben in for a hug. "It's not your fault, son. It's his. Every time we start to close in on his dog-fighting ring, he shuts things down for a while. But thanks to you and Noah, we're closer to getting him than we've ever been." He gently pulled back so he could look his son in the eye. "You put yourself—and your friend—in some serious danger, Ben," his dad said quietly but seriously. "And we're going to have to deal with the choices you made."

"I know."

"But first, let's find Mitch. I'll call this new information in to the station."

He stepped away and talked on his cell for a few minutes, then came back.

"The entire department is out there looking," his dad said. "And now they have more information to help them. That's going to make this go a lot faster."

"That's great, Dad."

"Go on up to do your homework, Ben," his dad said.

"What? No!" Ben cried out. "But I can help—I'm the only person who's been to his house!"

"If this Mitch guy knows what you look like—" his dad started to say. He shook his head, as if he couldn't even finish the sentence. "I know it's hard, Ben, but we just need to let my guys do their jobs."

"Come on, honey," his mom said. "It's been a long couple of days."

"I can't just sit around and do nothing!" Ben jammed his hands into his sweatshirt pockets in frustration.

"Ben." His dad folded his arms across his chest and leaned back in his chair. He looked at the ceiling, like he was thinking about something very carefully. Then he reached out and put a hand on Ben's shoulder.

"I never said we'd do nothing," his dad said. "But you're not going to find him." Ben was crushed. "*We're* going out to find him. Together." Ben's dad looked at his wife. "Honey, I'll send a uniformed officer to stay outside the house until I get back."

She didn't look happy about it, but she nodded.

"Keep him safe," she said to her husband.

"Always."

She turned to Ben and gave him a kiss.

"Keep him safe," she said, nodding in the direction of his dad.

"I promise, Mom," Ben said.

"We'll start by trying to find our way back to Mitch's house," Ben's dad said to him. "Let's go."

"Hey, Dad—I'm actually not the one who can get us back to Mitch's house," Ben said quietly.

"Ben, what do you mean? You just asked—" His dad gave him a confused took.

"Hero." Ben said. "Hero's the one who led me there the first time. We have to take him with us." At the sound of his name, Hero got to his feet and limped over to them. He sat down next to Ben, his front legs perfectly aligned, his ears up and at attention.

"Ben, Hero's under doctor's orders to rest."

"I know. But he's our best hope."

Ben's dad opened his mouth to speak, then closed it again. He threw his hands up in the air.

"You're right, son. Hero is our only chance of finding this guy. But he needs a scent item to track Mitch. Last time Hero had Scout's scent, remember?"

Ben's face lit up. "Will this do?" he asked, pulling a torn scrap of denim from his sweatshirt pocket. He'd forgotten all about it until just a moment ago. It was the piece of Mitch's jeans that Hero had ripped off when he bit him. Ben had pulled it from Hero's mouth when he and Noah had picked up the injured dog. Ben must have stuffed it in his pocket without realizing it.

"Is that from Mitch?" his dad asked, astonished.

Ben nodded.

"Wait here," his dad said. He ran upstairs and came back down with a black nylon dog vest, marked with K-9 UNIT in neon yellow. Ben's dad gently placed it over Hero's back and buckled it around his chest. Ben and his parents beamed at Hero. He looked so distinguished in his uniform—like the courageous police dog he had been for so many years. "He's your dog now," Ben's dad said to Ben. "He's under your command."

"Hero, let's go," Ben said, speaking with authority, like Officer Perillo had taught him. Hero stood at attention by Ben's left side. Ben started walking toward the door. Hero limped along with him, but as soon as he got close to Scout, he sat down again. "Hero—let's go," Ben repeated. "I swear, I've been working with him a lot, Dad, and he's never done this before."

"It's not you," Ben's dad said, shaking his head in disbelief. "It's Scout. He won't come without him."

At the sound of Scout's name, Hero barked once.

"Hang on," Ben's dad said. He ran upstairs again and came back down with a smaller vest. "This was Hero's when he first started out." It was big on Scout as Ben's dad strapped it onto the puppy, but it would work.

"Hero, Scout," Ben said, "let's go!"

24

SCOUT JUMPED AROUND EXCITEDLY ON BEN'S lap while
Hero rested on the backseat of Ben's dad's police cruiser.
Ben told his dad to drive to the outskirts of town, off
Highway 49, to the last spot Ben remembered from that day.

They pulled over at a rural intersection where, just
ahead of them, three narrow roads came together. Ben
looked down each of the roads and willed himself to
remember which way he and Hero had gone. Nothing.

They climbed out of the car. Ben opened the back
door for Hero, who got out with a little pained wince.
Ben put Scout down on the ground. He looked at his
dad, who nodded.

"Okay, Hero. Are you ready?" Ben held the piece

of Mitch's jeans under Hero's nose. Hero sniffed and exhaled, sniffed and exhaled. After a few minutes, Ben breathed in deep, filling his diaphragm with air. "Hero, find it!" he said in his most commanding voice.

Hero sniffed at the ground. He sniffed at the breeze and bobbed his head up and down with the air currents. Then he took off at what was, for him, a reasonable pace. Hero couldn't run, but he walked quickly, favoring his sore leg. Ben and his dad were able to keep up, while Scout's little legs worked double time as he ran along at Hero's side.

They walked down a quiet road with very few houses on it. Horses grazed behind fences along their route, but Hero was too focused on tracking to notice. His entire body moved in one fluid motion, following an invisible trail. He stayed totally on task, even as his ears twitched at the sounds of chirping birds and planes passing overhead.

They came to another road, leading off at an angle to the right. Without hesitation, Hero led them to the right.

"Good boy," Ben said.

They continued on for what must have been a couple of miles, through several turns, until they were in an isolated residential neighborhood. Ben noticed more on foot than he had while riding his bike through here the other day. The houses were set far apart from each other, and the streets were quiet. There were no kids playing on the lawns. No neighbors waved at each other over hedges. The area felt deserted. It gave Ben the creeps.

He looked over at his dad. His face was serious, and he studied their surroundings carefully. His hand rested on his gun holster. Ben could tell he was in police mode. Ben felt so much safer having his dad there with him.

Soon, they found themselves on a street with only a couple of houses on it. This was starting to feel familiar to Ben. Scout barked a few times as they rounded a slight curve, and Ben saw it: A hundred yards up on the right was Mitch's house. The SUV was in the driveway.

They were there. Hero had done it.

Ben's heart picked up speed in his chest. His hands were clammy. Could Mitch really be in there? He had no idea what they were about to find.

"That's it, Dad," Ben said quietly, pointing at the house. They stopped walking. Ben's dad squinted and surveyed the house carefully.

Hero's whole demeanor grew even more focused and alert. He scanned the street and the handful of houses on the block. His face was neutral, unreadable. He stood with his back straight, his shoulders down, and his body ready for action.

Ben picked up Scout and gave both dogs a treat from his jeans pocket.

All the windows and doors of Mitch's house were shut. The street was totally silent.

"Listen to me, Ben," his dad said, his voice low. "I know how you feel about this guy. Believe me—he tried to hurt you. No one wants to catch him as much as I do. But we need to be safe about this, okay?"

Ben nodded.

"I need to get a look at that license plate," his dad said. He walked quickly and quietly so he could get a clear view of the house and car. Ben hustled after him, Hero walking close to his side and Scout safely resting in his arms. They stopped behind a tall hedge just past the house.

Ben's dad pulled out his cell phone. He tracked their location on his GPS, dropped a dot on the map, and called the station.

"Sheridan, it's Landry," he said quietly into the phone. "I'm at the suspect's possible location. Address is . . ."

Ben squatted down behind the hedge and peered through it toward the house. From that angle, he had a view of the driveway that ran along the house to a backyard. It was getting dark. Shadows had started to fall across the roof.

A curtain moved in a side window. Ben sucked in his breath. Someone was in the house.

"Dad—" he whispered.

". . . tell them to get here as fast as they can. Southeast corner. Vehicle is here. House appears to be empty but have not confirmed whether suspect is inside."

The curtain parted farther, then quickly fell closed again.

"Dad!"

Ben's dad gestured for him to wait.

"That's right. Delta Alpha Tango. Right. Niner . . ." He held up a finger to Ben, telling him to wait one more second.

Still holding Scout, Ben slipped farther along the hedge, toward the house.

"Hang on," his dad said into the phone. "Ben, what're you doing?" he whispered loudly. "Stay here. They're five minutes out."

Ben kept walking.

"We're not going in without backup," his dad said.

Ben stopped. His dad started talking into the phone again. Through an opening in the hedge, Ben had a better angle on the house. He studied the window, waiting for something to happen. Then, it did. The curtain moved aside, and someone looked out the window and nervously surveyed the street. Ben gasped. It was a familiar face: It was Mitch.

"Dad—I see him," Ben said over his shoulder.

His dad spoke urgently into the phone.

"Sheridan, we have a visual on the suspect. Repeat: We have a visual on the suspect. We've got to get in there. They need to double-time it!"

25

IT ALL HAPPENED SO FAST. SCOUT leaped from Ben's arms, landed lightly on the ground, and bolted at top speed toward the house.

Without thinking, Ben ran after him.

"Ben!" his dad yelled. "Stop!"

Ben couldn't stop. Not when Scout was headed for danger. There was no telling what Mitch would do to Scout if he saw him again—after all, it was Scout who had brought down Mitch's dogfighting ring. It was a safe bet that Mitch wasn't feeling too fond of Scout at the moment.

Scout darted around the house, into the backyard. Ben followed him. He came around the back corner just in time to see Scout slip through a narrow opening in a sliding glass door. The puppy disappeared into the house. Ben grabbed the door and slid it open enough to fit through. Before he could go in, though, Hero ran up from behind him and dashed through the opening after Scout.

The house was dark inside. Scout was nowhere to be seen. Ben and Hero stepped quietly forward. They crossed a darkened room, then turned into a long hallway. There, at the far end, where the hallway opened up into a large living room, was Scout. He stood with his back to them. His whole body was shaking.

"Scout, come," Ben whispered. But Scout didn't move. He didn't even turn around. He was focused on something that Ben and Hero couldn't see—and he was paralyzed with fear. At Ben's side, Hero picked up on a scent and started to growl.

Then Ben heard a very unwelcome noise: a guttural, nasty snarling from not one but two very angry dogs, around the corner from where Scout stood. Before Ben could stop him, Hero took off down the hallway and headed straight into the room where the dogs were. The sickening sounds of a vicious fight rang out almost instantly.

Ben ran toward the fight. Scout stood off to the side barking frantically, while Hero and the two dogs spun in circles, snapping their jaws and pouncing on each other. It was a cloud of fur and spit.

"Hero, no!" Ben shouted. But there was no stopping him. Hero was going to fight those dogs with everything he had—he would die to protect Scout, and Ben knew it.

"What the heck's going on out there?" Ben heard a man's voice yell from the other side of a swinging door, which Ben figured was the kitchen. Limping footsteps thumped in their direction. Mitch had heard the commotion—and he was coming for them. Ben had to get his dogs out of there, and fast.

Scout skittered back and forth around the fight, barking and whining. Ben watched in horror as, suddenly, Scout ran right into the middle of the battle.

"No—Scout!" Ben screamed.

Mitch's footsteps grew louder.

"Ben?" His dad had come in through the back of the house and was heading for them.

It was all happening at once.

The chaos of the fight grew louder with one more animal in the ring. Ben heard Scout cry out in pain, then saw Hero bite down on one of the other dogs in response.

All of a sudden, Scout zipped out from the scrum and took off toward the sound of Mitch's footsteps. At the same moment, the kitchen door swung open, and Mitch appeared, his face lit up with rage. Scout scurried between his legs and ran—faster than Ben had ever seen him move—into the kitchen. One of Mitch's dogs broke away from the fight and chased after him. The bigger dog was fast on Scout's tail, barking fiercely. Hero ran after them, followed closely by the second dog.

The sound faded as the door swung shut behind them. Ben could hear the muffled noises of their on-going fight.

"Hello again," Mitch said, a cold sneer on his face.

"Ben—are you okay?" His dad was right behind him, his service revolver in his hand. He quickly took in the scene.

"I see you brought backup today, huh, Ben?" Mitch said. He looked from one to the other. There was a hole in Mitch's jeans and bloodstains where Hero had bitten him. The wound was clearly bad, but there was no way Mitch could show his face at a hospital or doctor's office with a dog bite like that on his leg. Not when the whole police force was out looking for him.

Ben's dad stepped forward and positioned himself between Mitch and Ben.

"I wouldn't do that," Mitch said, his voice laced with hostility.

Ben's dad eyed Mitch up and down, sizing him up. "You need to leave my son alone, Mitch."

Mitch let out a nasty cackle. "Do I? Maybe you're the one who needs to keep a better eye on him."

"I've got my eye on you now, and that's all that matters," Ben's dad said. Mitch took an uneven step toward Ben's dad.

"Dad!" Ben cried.

"It's okay, Ben," he replied without taking his eyes off Mitch.

Sirens wailed in the distance. Mitch's eyes hardened.

Ben's dad slid his gun into its holster. He held up his hands to show Mitch that they were empty.

"Look, Mitch—I've put away my gun," Ben's dad said, his voice calm and matter-of-fact. "My son is here, and I don't want anyone to get hurt. Backup will be here any second. You'd be crazy to do anything stupid right now."

"What do I have to lose?" Mitch countered.

Ben heard a stampede of animals headed back toward them. Just as Mitch registered the sound, Scout and Hero came blasting into the room from behind him. Scout scuttled through Mitch's legs, and Hero slipped around him. They stopped by Ben and his dad. Mitch's two dogs skidded into the room, their nails scratching on the hardwood floor. The dogs barreled around Mitch and cornered Ben, his dad, Hero, and Scout.

"Good dogs," Mitch said. He grinned at Ben. "Gotcha now, kid."

The dogs snarled at Hero and Scout. Hero lowered himself into a fighting stance. Scout crouched down by Ben's side and barked back at them. The sound of the sirens grew louder. Mitch took another menacing step toward them.

"What's it gonna be, Mitch?" Ben's dad asked.

Mitch lurched forward, favoring his good leg. His miserable face was screwed up in an angry scowl.

He opened his mouth to speak, but before he could get a word out, Scout launched himself at Mitch. The puppy jumped onto Mitch's wounded leg, closing his small but sharp teeth on his calf. Mitch bellowed in agony, his eyes practically popping out of his head from

205

the pain. He tried to shake Scout off, but Scout clamped his jaws more tightly, wrapped his paws around Mitch's leg, and held on for dear life.

Mitch spun around in a circle, flailing his arms. Hero saw an opening and flung himself forward, knocking Mitch backward to the ground—where he landed on top of his demonic dogs. The dogs howled in pain and tried to wriggle out from underneath him, but Mitch was too big. Scout was still gnawing on his leg, and Hero had them all pinned. Mitch writhed in misery.

The sirens were right outside. Four cops in uniform—and one K-9, the Akita that Ben had seen at the training course—burst into the room. The officers pointed their guns at Mitch. One of them stepped forward and cuffed him. As she did, she looked over at Ben.

"You okay, Ben?" It was Officer Perillo.

Ben nodded.

It was over.

"Hero, Scout, come," Ben called out.

Hero hobbled toward Ben. Ben could tell that his leg was hurting him. Scout released his grip on Mitch's leg and scurried over too. Ben picked him up. He squatted down so he could hug both dogs at once. He buried his face in Hero's neck, then into Scout's fur.

"You did it, guys," Ben said to them. "You saved us."

Ben's dad wrapped his arms around Ben and the dogs. "You guys okay?"

Ben nodded.

"You were all very brave," Ben's dad said. "I'm proud of you."

"Thanks," Ben muttered. Relief washed over him. Mitch was headed to jail. Hero and Scout were safe.

Ben's dad put a hand on Hero's head. "Hero, you've never failed me once. There will never be another dog like you. You're truly a lifesaver." Then he put his hand under Scout's tiny chin and tilted his head upward. "And you, mister." Ben's dad gave the puppy a long look. "You're one fine dog."

Perillo had Mitch up on his feet, hands cuffed behind his back. The officers led him and his dogs out of the room.

"You're under arrest . . ." Ben heard Perillo say as they headed down the hall.

Ben looked around the room. His heart swelled with gratitude and pride—for his dad, Scout, and Hero.

He was the luckiest kid on earth.

26

HERO LIMPED ACROSS THE KITCHEN FLOOR while Scout yipped at his heels and scurried around him. About halfway across the room, Hero stopped. Scout stopped too and gazed up at the bigger dog. Hero lowered his nose and nudged Scout on the belly, knocking him over and rolling him onto his back. Scout wagged his tail and licked Hero on the nose.

"Hey, Ben," his dad said, "hand me those burger buns, would you?"

"I got it, Mr. Landry," Noah replied, snatching up the package from the counter and tossing it to him.

"Nice arm, Noah." Ben's dad grinned. "You getting ready for the season?"

"I'm ready! If it were up to me, there wouldn't be an off-season."

"You've been warned, boys," Ben's mom joked. "No one will be cheering louder than us."

Ben shook his head and grinned.

"I believe you, Mom."

Ben had barely had time to think about it: He was going to be the starting shortstop. On the varsity team. Practice started in a few days. It had been his dream for so long that it still didn't seem real.

Coach had called Ben that morning to talk about his expectations for the season. On the phone, Ben had asked him about Jack.

"I'm not sure Jack is ready to be part of our team," Coach had said. Ben didn't know what he was going to say until the words were already out of his mouth.

"Coach, I know this isn't any of my business," Ben said. "But do you think you could give Jack another chance?"

"I'm surprised to hear you say that, Landry," Coach replied. "And why do you think I should do that? After all, you're the one who got hit with the ball."

"I know. But I think—I mean, I think Jack has just been having a really hard time. He's new in town, and he didn't really have anyone to help him out. Maybe he just had a bad day. We all do sometimes, right?"

Coach chuckled. "I guess we do, Ben. I guess we do. Okay, I'll consider it. I haven't quite figured out what to do with first base. And he's got a good arm."

"Thanks, Coach. I really appreciate it."

"Well,"—Ben's mom interrupted his thoughts, nudging past him with a tray of hamburger patties—"it seems like we have a lot to celebrate around here, doesn't it?"

"We sure do," his dad chimed in. "Including the fact that you've got another great dog on your hands, Ben." He pointed at Scout, who was now playing a competitive game of hide-and-seek with Erin. Scout was gnawing on a squeaky chew toy, and Erin took it away from him to hide it. Scout sat patiently and waited for Erin to give him the *find it* command.

"Erin, honey," his dad said with a laugh, "if Scout watches you hide the toy, he knows where it is."

"He's still the best puppy ever!" she squealed.

The doorbell rang. Ben's parents looked at each other.

"You expecting someone?" his mom asked. His dad shook his head.

"Actually," Ben said, "it's for me." He opened the

door. It was Jack. "I think you guys know Jack Murphy. Jack, this is . . . my family."

"Hi, everyone," Jack said with a shy wave.

"Come on in, Jack," Ben's mom said, leading him into the kitchen. "I hope you're hungry."

"Yes, ma'am, I am," Jack said.

Ben swallowed, trying to clear the lump in his throat. "There's, um, something I wanted to tell you guys about Scout," he said softly.

The room went quiet. Ben's mom and dad fixed their eyes on their son, worried expressions on both their faces. Ben couldn't blame them—he and the dogs had given them plenty to worry about recently.

"It's nothing bad. Don't worry!" Ben said. His parents visibly relaxed. "It's just . . ." This was harder to say out loud than he'd expected. It was a decision he'd played out in his mind dozens of times, running it backward and forward until he was sure it was the right thing to do. And it was the right thing to do. It just wasn't going to be easy.

Ben swallowed and waited a moment until he knew his voice would be steady when he spoke. Everyone was watching him, waiting. "I knew as soon as Hero and I found Scout in the woods that he was something special. And Hero really thinks so too. Scout has come so far. He's not the scared little guy he was a few weeks ago. He's a . . . well, he's a hero!"

Everyone laughed. Ben forced himself to go on.

"And I think he deserves a really happy home, where he will get as much love and attention as he can handle. Which is a lot." Ben looked at Jack, whose eyes were wide open in surprise. "And a home that's close by so we can see him all the time, right, Hero?"

Hero let out a short howl. Ben looked at Noah, who gave him an encouraging nod. Ben's parents were teary. Ben had to look away from them so he didn't lose it.

"Jack," Ben said, "I really want you to have Scout. I know he can't replace Holly, but he's pretty great."

Jack's mouth fell open. "Really?" He gasped. "I'm sorry that I was so mean to you before, but I think maybe I do just need a new friend. Thank you."

Ben nodded. "I already talked to your mom about it. She's totally cool with it."

Ben's mom let out a little surprised "Oh my!" His dad smiled broadly.

Erin squealed, "You can't give my puppy to someone else, Benny!"

"No—it's okay, Erin. We'll still get to visit him, okay?"

Erin burst into tears. "Okay," she choked out between sobs. Ben's dad picked her up and comforted her.

"Wow—I don't even know what to—I mean— wow . . ." Jack stammered. "Thank you, thank you, Ben!" Jack summoned Scout over. The puppy ran right up to him. Jack picked Scout up, and immediately the puppy started to lick Jack's nose, ears, and cheeks.

"I think Scout is happy about it," Ben said.

Ben was enveloped in a massive hug by his parents and Erin. The group broke apart at the sound of barking and whining. Hero and Scout wedged their way into the center of the huddle, tails wagging.

"Come on in, guys," Ben said, laughing. He dropped to his knees on the kitchen floor. Scout hopped up on his lap, and Hero nuzzled Ben with his snout.

"We're going to miss you, Scout," Ben said, holding the pup's face in his hands. Scout licked Ben's nose. "Thanks for everything, pal."

Ben put his arms around the dogs. He had never felt so sure of anything before.

27

BEN NARROWED HIS EYES AND FOCUSED on the ball. He pushed away everything else—the cheering and clapping, the sound of his parents shouting his name, Hero's excited barking, Scout's sharp yapping. Ben breathed in, out, in, out. It was just him, the pitcher, and the ball. Ben's hands were relaxed on the bat as he held it high behind his head. He bobbed up and down on his knees, readying his muscles to run to first base . . . or even farther.

And then, it all happened at once, in a fluid sequence of events that seemed like a perfectly coordinated dance: The ball left the pitcher's hand, Ben released his swing, the bat let out a deep, rich crack as it connected with the ball, Ben dropped the bat and launched himself toward first base, then second as he watched the ball sail toward center field and heard it land in the grass.

He stopped at second base and looked toward the bleachers. His mom and dad hooted and hollered. Erin jumped up and down on the bench, holding Hero's leash in her small hand. Hero, who had a new bandage on his leg, woofed a couple of times and wagged his tail. Jack's mom was there too, holding Scout in her arms so he could see the game. Scout barked and barked until everyone around them on the benches laughed, and Jack's mom shushed him.

Ben shook out his arms, staying loose and ready to run. From the corners of his eyes, he took note of where every player in the infield was. He spotted Noah in the dugout, stretching. Ben turned his attention to the next play, ready to focus on the batter who stepped up to the plate. It was Jack. Ben gave him a thumbs-up, and Jack nodded back.

The pitcher released the ball, and Jack sent it sailing far over Ben's head, perfectly angled between the center- and left-fielders. Ben rounded the corner at third base, and headed for home plate. Once he was safe, he turned to see Jack coming around third, then heading toward him. Home run!

Ben high-fived Jack as he pounded his foot on the base and slowed himself to a stop. Ben's and Jack's families were going nuts in the bleachers. As the cheering died down, Ben heard Scout howl long and loud, and Hero let out a series of happy barks.

It's going to be a great season, Ben thought. *With Hero, Scout, Noah, and Jack on my team . . . we can do anything.*

ACKNOWLEDGMENTS

Boundless thanks to Les Morgenstein, Josh Bank, Sara Shandler, and the amazing Alloy team, and Margaret Anastas, Nicole Hoff, and everyone on the Harper sales, marketing, and publicity teams. Huge gratitude to Robin Straus, Katelyn Hales, and Gracie, as well as Virginia Wing, Kunsang Bhuti, and Stacey Silverman. Plus extra special tail wags to Hayley Wagreich, the Hero of book editors.